Additional Praise for

STRONG LIKE YOU

"I love Walker Lauderdale, this kid so angry—with every right to be angry—who takes it all out on the football field. He has this great courage that drives him forward into danger and truth, but also, eventually, into acceptance and the space to be moved by the love around him. Walker is so much more than some poor kid, more than a linebacker to be feared, more than a footnote in a rural tragedy. In his coming of age, he becomes graceful. This is a hell of a book."

—Geoff Herbach, author of *Stupid Fast* and *Hooper*

"A well-executed story by a dynamic and riveting writer. Take notice—T. L. Simpson has arrived."

—Paul Volponi, multi-award-winning, best-selling author of *Black and White*, *Rikers High*, *The Final Four*, and *Superhero Smart*

"T. L. Simpson's emotionally charged coming-of-age tale drags all five of the reader's senses across hot coals as troubled teen linebacker Walker Lauderdale struggles to cope with the searing aftermath of a hard-hearted father who has mysteriously vanished. The author's choice to bring Walker's story to life via a flinty, first-person, present-tense monologue is nothing short of genius."

—Craig Leener, author of *There's No Basketball on Mars*

"*Strong Like You* is a twisty and thought-provoking mystery I can't stop thinking about. In his engaging debut novel, T. L. Simpson takes an unflinching and insightful look at boyhood, masculinity, and what it truly means to be 'strong.' His vulnerable characters and enchanting prose are a breath of fresh air, making this book relatable, slightly gut-wrenching, and absolutely impossible to put down. I know I'll be sharing this one with all the young people in my life!"

—Emily Bleeker, ͏ ͏ ͏ of
ͽne

STRONG LIKE YOU

T. L. SIMPSON

Mendota Heights, Minnesota

First Edition
First Printing, 2024

Book design by Cynthia Della-Rovere
Cover design by Cynthia Della-Rovere
Cover illustration by Caitlin O'Dwyer

Flux, an imprint of North Star Editions, Inc.

Library of Congress Cataloging-in-Publication Data
Names: Simpson, T. L., author.
Title: Strong like you / T. L. Simpson.
Description: First edition. | Mendota Heights, Minnesota : Flux, 2024. | Audience: Grades 10-12.
Identifiers: LCCN 2023040094 (print) | LCCN 2023040095 (ebook) | ISBN 9781635830941 (paperback) | ISBN 9781635830958 (ebook)
Subjects: CYAC: Identity--Fiction. | Fathers and sons--Fiction. | Missing persons--Fiction. | LCGFT: Novels.
Classification: LCC PZ7.1.S5655 St 2024 (print) | LCC PZ7.1.S5655 (ebook) | DDC [Fic]--dc23
LC record available at https://lccn.loc.gov/2023040094
LC ebook record available at https://lccn.loc.gov/2023040095

Flux
North Star Editions, Inc.
2297 Waters Drive
Mendota Heights, MN 55120
www.fluxnow.com

For Greg, Kaylee, Jeffrey, and Henry

I haven't cried one time since you disappeared. Not even at football practice when Paton Roper told the whole team you were probably dead. He said, "You know how sometimes a dog gets sick or bites somebody and you have to put it down?"

Somebody said, "Yep."

"That's probably what happened to Walker's daddy."

Some people laughed. Others turned away like they ain't heard nothing. Paton said he knew that kind of thing since his father's the Ike County sheriff. Paton looks like the quarterback in every movie ever made about football. Blond hair. Blue eyes. Muscles everywhere. He looks tough, but there's one thing I know that he don't: Muscles don't make you strong. Strength is in your brain. In your blood. In the way you are hardened by the things around you. Some folks got it soft, but I am not one of those people.

Truth is, what Paton said don't bother me much. Because I know something else he don't.

You ain't dead.

There's *no way* you're dead.

There's no way someone strong like you is gone forever and don't nobody even know about it.

1

Ain't nobody take this serious—getting ready for a game. They look around at each other, make jokes, blast music real loud, and act stupid. I put on my shoulder pads, tighten the straps under my arms, and don't say nothing. Old Coach let this shit slide. But our new one ain't the type. Letting small stuff slide is how you end up with back-to-back winless seasons. And if you're Old Coach, it's how you end up getting run out of your job.

The door to the locker room flies open, and Coach Widner steps inside, blowing his whistle so loud it hurts my ears. Someone cranks down the stereo, and we stand there in all different states of dress and undress.

Coach Widner runs a brown hand over his mouth, smoothing out his mustache. "What is this? What are we doing?" He walks up and down the aisles, his hands on his hips, a frown on his face. "Why are we grab-assing around when we got a game to win?"

Coach Widner took over our program last offseason. Moved here from Mississippi for the job. Held a parent-player meeting the first week, and told every person there his aim was to turn our losing program around. His goal was simple: to win football games and build better men. Take a guess which of those two got cheers from the crowd.

When the parent meeting was over, someone said to you, "A black feller, huh?"

And you said, "He could be a blue kangaroo for all I care. Long as he wins football games."

At first, I didn't give a damn about who our coach was, but when you went missing, he started coming to the house "to check up" on me. He's been coming by almost every day, and every day he talks to me less and talks to Momma more.

Does he think I'm stupid?

Does he think I don't know what he's doing?

What does he think will happen when you come home?

I've put up with it about as long as I can handle.

"You boys think you are ready?" he says, patrolling up and down the locker room, his bald head already pebbled with sweat. "Think you're going to loaf around before the game, then go out there and win? Let me tell you something. It doesn't work like that. Not in my locker room. Not in my football program. Don't talk. Don't play grab ass. Don't do nothing but *focus*. This is *War Eagles* football."

Sawyer Metcalf gets dressed across the room. His daddy, Rufus, gone missing same time you did, almost a month ago now. Which makes sense because y'all are always running together. From the start, I figure you two was out cutting loose somewhere, getting up to who knows what kind of trouble. I like to think about you and him getting up to no good. Like Wild West cowboys. Hootin' and hollerin', I bet. I laugh anytime I think about it. You two was friends since you was little. Friends who married sisters. Sisters who got pregnant at the same time and had boys—me and Sawyer. Cousins who growed up together from the start. Who never stopped backing each other up. Who became little versions of you and Rufus. On and off the football field.

Sawyer catches me looking. He grins his crooked, missing-tooth smile, tucks a strand of his long, blond hair behind an ear. "Focus, Walker," he says, a laugh hidden somewhere behind his words.

Coach Widner scowls at him. "You can leave if you don't like it."

Sawyer's eyes widen. "Sorry, sir."

Coach Widner stares at him for a long time. Then he keeps walking. When he leaves the room, I pull my jersey over my shoulder pads and walk over to Sawyer. "You think our dads will show up tonight?"

Sawyer turns away from me, acts like he is looking for something in his locker, but all his shit is on the bench behind him. There ain't a thing in the world inside that locker he could be looking for. "They wouldn't miss it, Walker. Ain't no way they'd miss our first game."

When we're dressed, Coach Widner leads us to the field, his bald head steaming in the cold air. Some cheerleaders inflate a gigantic orange-and-blue football helmet with the word SAMSON printed on the side. More cheerleaders hold a paper sign that says *SLAY THOSE DRAGONS* across the front.

We huddle together inside the helmet, and I look down at myself in my War Eagles uniform.

I have waited so long for this moment.

Waited so long to step on that field.

To play football on Friday nights.

To wear the same uniform you once wore.

To burst out of that helmet and through that paper sign.

Someone, Paton maybe, starts a chant. It starts low and slow and builds like fire growing. Before long, we yell it together.

"BLOOD.

"BLOOD.

"BLOOD MAKES THE GRASS GROW."

We jump up and down.

"BLOOD."

Shoulder pads thumping.

"BLOOD."

Helmets scraping.

"BLOOD MAKES THE GRASS GROW."

The whole time I wonder . . . are you out there? Somewhere in the stands? Waiting for me to burst through this helmet and take the field for my first varsity football game?

The band plays the fight song. Someone lets loose with a fire extinguisher. And we come pouring through the front of the facemask, emerging from the smoke, tearing through paper, thundering down the sideline.

I look up at the stands.

I scan every seat, hoping to find you.

Sawyer comes from behind me. "You see them anywhere?"

"Nope."

"God damn."

It don't make sense, you missing my first game. I know you were looking forward to it. It was all you talked about for a while. You drove me to practice all summer, dropped me off in our old, beat-up Dodge Ram truck, blue paint faded on the hood into gray and rust, Arkansas Razorbacks sticker on the back glass. And when I come off that practice field, there you were. Every time. Waiting in the parking lot. Country music playing too loud through the rolled-down windows.

You said football made you the man you are today. And you said it would do that to me too. When I was little, I used to ask if you'd read to me before bed. You'd always put down your beer and say something like, "Sure thing, Walker. I'll be back there in a minute." But I always fell asleep before you showed up. The more I think about it, I could hardly get you to show up for anything. Except football. You showed up for football.

But not tonight.

So when they blow the whistle to start the game, I check the stands one more time. Just to be sure. Think maybe you'll sneak in the back. Stand near the top. Look down on me like *surprise, Walker, I'm here. And I ain't leaving. Let's play some football.*

Steelville lines up against us. Bunch of little boys from the hills a county over. Sawyer takes his spot at the "Will" linebacker spot. That's the weak side. You'd be proud to see us there. Anchors on the defense. Me and my cousin. Sawyer, the son of your best friend in the whole world. Momma's nephew. And me. Your blood. Out there on the field. Just like you when you were my age.

I reach out and slap Sawyer's hand before the first snap. Coach Widner makes a hand motion like he is throwing a lasso. "Rodeo, rodeo," he yells. "Let's hit them in the mouth, set the tone for this game!"

Sawyer grins at me. Rodeo is our favorite blitz.

Their center hikes the ball, and we crash the "A" gaps. There ain't a fat lineman from Steelville can block either of us. We break into the backfield and there he is, little skinny Steelville quarterback, number twelve on his jersey, with not a soul to protect him. He curls his back away from us, afraid of the hit. Me on one side. Sawyer on the other. The whole world quiet. Waiting for the moment. The crunch.

Our shoulder pads and helmets sandwich this boy between us, and I hear the naked air come rushing from his lungs. We hit the ground in a heap. Legs tangled. Arms tangled. Steelville quarterback starts moaning before I can stand up. A ref separates us on the ground. He takes one look at the quarterback, and his face turns as green as a moldy apple. He blows his whistle and waves for the other officials. The quarterback groans. Lifts his leg.

Then he screams.

His leg is broken through the middle of the shin. Like a twig somebody stepped on. Looks like nothing but his sock is keeping his foot from falling off.

We take a knee, Sawyer next to me. He pinches the back of my calf to get my attention. He whispers, "That happen to me, I'd be up ready for the next play already."

"With a broken leg?" I say, trying not to laugh.

Sawyer grins crooked. He is missing one front tooth that never growed in, or maybe got knocked out somehow and I never heard about it. "Limp right into the end zone, whole team on my back."

The ambulance drives onto the field, throwing red and blue strobes over everything, like the lights outside my bedroom so many times. I think of you on the porch, arguing and cussing, some poor deputy trying to talk you down from something stupid. The more I picture you bowed up against the law, Momma and I watching scared from the kitchen window, the more I think if you had found the time to come to this game, you would have been proud of me. Proud of your boy. Proud if you'd seen it. Seen me hit the quarterback so hard he broke his leg.

But you ain't here.

And I got to chew on that.

But I ain't about to cry. No way. Not even one tear will leak from these eyes. 'Cause you told me. Told me from the day I was a baby. Men like us, we don't cry. We don't ever show weakness. We're strong, I can hear you saying it, *we're strong, Walker, strong because we got no choice. Strong because this world will crush you if you ain't. Strong because there ain't no other way for a man to be.*

Bellwork
In the space below, describe your favorite high school experience
so far.

_____

~~I to~~ the only good thing about high school is ~~football~~. I am starting linebacker. Not a lot of Sophomores get ~~—~~ to start. But I do. And so does my cousin Sawyer. We both play linebacker.

2

There's a new girl in my English class. I do my bellwork, these little writing assignments Mrs. Redman hands out every day, then I put my head on my desk. I turn to one side and close my eyes so it'll look like I am sleeping, but I open them just enough to see New Girl between the cracks.

She has a notebook open on her desk, writing something down the center of the page before class gets going.

"We have a new student," Mrs. Redman says. Then, to the girl, "Why don't you tell everyone your name and where you're from and what brought you here to Samson."

New Girl looks around. Her eyes are wide, and I can tell she's scared. She closes the notebook on her desk, and I see the front says *Creative Writing, Fifth Period, Mrs. Wells.*

I don't know what creative writing is, but something about the scared look on her face makes me feel sorry for her. Makes me *like* her. The thing I like about her best is that she don't know me. Every person in Samson has some idea of who I am.

They all think, *That's Hank Lauderdale's boy, Walker.*

Walker's poor as shit.

Dumb as rocks.

Rotten as his father.

I can't escape these things. These ideas. They're as ingrained as quartz in the hills of the Ozarks. So I like New Girl, her black hair and green eyes, splatter of freckles across her cheeks, nose small and turned up on the end, with a little silver loop between her nostrils. I like all those things. But mostly, I like that she doesn't have some big idea on who I'm supposed to be.

"My name is Chloe Ennis," she says. "We moved here from New York."

"New York, wow," Mrs. Redman said.

And I think the same thing. *Wow, New York City.* I seen it in movies, but I can't imagine being someplace with buildings so tall you can't see the top from the bottom. I can't imagine people bustling shoulder to shoulder, so many you could get lost in them like a forest. I sit up. "You ever been on top the Empire State Building?"

Her cheeks turn red. She looks down at her desk. "Actually, I've never been in the city. I'm from Aurora. It's not that different from this place, really."

"Ain't all of New York a city?"

The class laughs. Chloe laughs too. For a second I feel embarrassed. Then I feel angry.

"What's funny?" I look around the room, daring someone to say something.

"New York is a state," Mrs. Redman says. "You're thinking of New York City, which is a big city in New York State."

I can feel the heat in my cheeks. I want to run out of the room. I hate the way she explains things to me. Like she thinks I might not be able to understand her. Like I am stupid.

Mrs. Redman moves on fast. "Open your books to page two hundred and . . ."

I put my head back on my desk. Pretend *none* of that ever happened.

The other boys' mommas pick them up in SUVs that glimmer in the sun like their fingernails on the steering wheels. They got makeup on. Shadows over their eyes, and red lips. I watch them while I wait on Sawyer, who is always slow to change clothes after football practice. I watch the spot where your truck would have been if you'd showed up this weekend like I told everybody you would.

The boys get into their mommas' cars, the cars their daddies bought their mommas, really. Mommas lean across and try and kiss them on the cheek. Watch them boys shrug away and give dirty looks. Too old for that shit. And those mommas don't get mad. They hand them water bottles and snacks.

Paton unchains a bike from the bike rack, then rides up and down the road popping wheelies off the curb. Then, he rides far away, pulls a U-turn, and pedals as hard as he can toward me. He stares straight at me, keeping those handlebars straight, that wheel pointed right at me. When he gets close, he slams the pedals backward. The tires bark on the asphalt. He puts his feet down and laughs. "Scared you."

"No, you didn't."

"I saw it in your face."

I ignore him.

"Walker."

I ignore him some more.

"Walker."

"What?"

"You like my new bike?"

A black-and-orange BMX. The kind for doing tricks. "Sure."

"I got one more year on two wheels, then Pa says I can get a truck. You gonna get a car, Walker?"

He knows the answer. He only asked to rub it in my face.

Just then, Sawyer comes outside, backpack slung over one shoulder.

"You ready?" he says, as if I ain't been waiting fifteen minutes. I am glad to see him. Glad to have a reason to walk away from Paton.

"Let's go," I say.

We walk across the middle school parking lot until we reach the sidewalk. Then we walk until the sidewalk crumbles away into tall grass.

"Your daddy turn up?" Sawyer asks me.

"Nope. Yours?"

"Nope."

"Hell."

I remember one time a long time ago you woke me up at one in the morning, dragged me out of bed and out the front door. Momma was asleep on the couch. Outside, Sawyer was with his daddy and another man I didn't know then but know now, Lukas Fisher. We all piled in your rusted-out truck and drove for an hour into the country, until we got to a house in the middle of nowhere, still under construction.

"Rufus," you said to Sawyer's daddy. "Let's be quick."

And he said back to you, "I know, Hank. Jesus."

I remember Rufus had a good job, even back then. That's one thing he always had you never did. A steady job. A *real* job. He worked at a chicken plant a county over, pulling the guts out of birds all night. He'd come home covered in blood and feathers, and I get why you ain't wanna do something like that. But the thing is, Sawyer always had food in his refrigerator. We borrowed from him half the time we run out. Other times we got from food pantries, or little boxes outside school or from church. Rest of the time, we just sat around and let our stomachs eat themselves.

Rufus had a job. He had some money. But he was always down to make a little more.

So me and you and Rufus and Sawyer and Lukas Fisher spent the next few hours pulling copper wiring out of the walls of that house. You showed me how to throw the breakers, to make sure I wouldn't get electrocuted. You showed me how to thread the wires through a plastic rod and secure it with electric tape, so we could pull the guts of the house out like a dead snake. You showed us how to strip the rubber so only the burnt-orange metal remained. How to spool it and throw it in the bed of the truck.

"What're we doing this for?" I asked you.

"A man paid me to do this," you said.

When the sun broke over the skeleton trees, and everything turned hot orange, we drove an hour to the city and the recycling place paid you two bucks per pound, which counted up to be two hundred dollars.

"There's like five hundred pounds of copper in some houses," you said. "That's food for a week, if you can get it all in a night."

I don't know why I remember this. Etched in my brain like Christmas morning. Waking up, not to open presents from Santa Claus, but to go with you into the woods and drink cold Dr Pepper while you sipped coffee and talked with Lukas and Rufus. Me and

Sawyer giggling like little crazy dogs in the bed of the truck, the cold wind whipping our hair wild as we flew down county roads in the dark.

It's a long walk home from school.

Plenty of time to think about these things.

"You think Lukas Fisher might know something about our dads?" I ask.

"Could be. Why?" Sawyer says.

"The last time we heard from Daddy was a text message he sent Momma."

"What'd he send?"

"A photo. Him, your daddy, and Lukas." Momma showed me the photo after you'd been gone a week. You in the center, your arms thrown around Rufus to your right and Lukas to your left, a longneck beer bottle dangling from one hand. Y'all looked happy, red-cheeked and drunk. Like best friends. I studied that picture hard, tried to remember every detail. You were in a bar, I know, because there was a neon-red sign behind you that said *Coors*. The whole place was wood and looked old, like a barrel left too long in the rain.

Sawyer kicks a rock, crams his hands into his jacket pockets. "Who knows, Walker. They was always running together."

We pass the elementary school, a little ramshackle building that reminds me of an old man with his shoulders slumped. There's a trailer across the street where some kids live. Two of them. We always see them playing on the rusted swing set in the schoolyard, their older brother watching over them.

But Older Brother isn't there. Not today. The kids are chasing each other, arguing over rules to some game they made up. Sawyer elbows me.

"Look here," he says. And I can hear the mischief in his voice. I'm good at hearing mischief in a voice.

The schoolyard is a muddy mess, with little crawdad mounds all over. I watch Sawyer pace around, his eyes sweeping across the grass. He seems to find what he is looking for because that mischief in his voice spreads all the way to his eyes. He gives me his crooked, missing-tooth smile, then reaches down and pins a crawdad between a finger and thumb.

"What are you doing?" I ask.

The kids notice us. They stop playing. The littlest one, wearing nothing but a pair of panties, hides behind her older sister's legs.

"What you got there?" the older girl says, sounding angry. Protective.

Sawyer holds up the mudbug. "You want to see?"

"Nope," the girl says, hands on her hips. "Them things give me the creeps."

Sawyer makes like he didn't hear her. He walks across the field, mud squishing around his shoes. "It won't hurt you."

"I don't like them," the girl says. She points to the smaller girl. "And Roo is scared to death of them."

Sawyer keeps walking.

The girls move in a circle away from him. "Get it out of here, I swear to God."

"Or what?" Sawyer says. He moves quickly toward them. The littlest girl, Roo, screams, and the sound is pure terror. Sawyer cackles like a coyote and jabs the bug toward her.

"Go away, you big asshole," the older girl screams.

But I knew soon as the words came out of her mouth, it would only make it worse.

"Alright," I say. I put a tone in my voice. The one you always used when you wanted me to stop cutting up. But Sawyer doesn't hear me. Doesn't act like he did, anyway. The little girl takes off running, and Sawyer goes after her. The oldest follows behind, cussing up a storm. By now, Older Brother is on the front porch. He dropped out of high school last year, I think. Would be a senior if he'd stayed. He is shirtless, with a cigarette in the corner of his mouth. Long, greasy hair on either side of his face. He scowls, and I know it's about to get bad for us.

"Sawyer, come on," I holler.

But he won't listen. One thing about Sawyer. He won't listen to nothing when he's having a good time. He won't listen to nothing when he's having a bad time, either. Pretty much, Sawyer won't listen to nothing anytime ever.

Older Brother hurries across the street. He flicks his cigarette in the road, dashing fire across the pavement. He whistles once, and both girls take his meaning immediately. They wheel in their path, zigzag around Sawyer and his crawdad, and beeline straight to their brother.

Sawyer turns and sees Older Brother. He plops the mudbug back on the ground and stuffs his hands in his pockets like he ain't done nothing wrong.

"I'm sorry," I say to Older Brother.

He glances down at me. His sisters slip their fingers into his hands.

"I tried to stop him," I say.

Older Brother doesn't say a word. Leaves me standing there feeling like the scum of the whole world. Like gum on the bottom of a sneaker and you're trying to play basketball.

On the way home, I thump my fist with one knuckle raised into Sawyer's shoulder. "Why'd you do that for?"

He winces when I hit him, but then he just shrugs. Reminds me of you, the way you would shrug after Momma scraped together all we had to bail you out of jail.

"Can't help myself sometimes, Walker," Sawyer says. "Really, I'm just full of life."

Full of life.

Full of shit, more like.

We walk another hour in silence. Kicking our feet. Stop in the Dollar General. We look at the movies and video games we cannot afford. Then, because we like to torture ourselves, we look at the cell phones too. After a while, Sawyer says, "Get us some snacks."

And I know what that means.

It's something we've done before. Usually, only when we are starving.

"I ain't that hungry," I tell him.

"Well, I am."

"You ain't got nothing at home?"

"Walker, stop being a sissy and help me."

Sawyer calls the store's only employee over and asks her all about the cell phones. "How do you get minutes on them? Do you got to sign anything? Which phone plays games the best?"

While he done that, I walk down the snack aisle and stuff food into my backpack. Whatever will fit. Candy bars. A few twenty-ounce sodas. MoonPies. A bag of corn chips.

Sawyer keeps that woman busy until I am standing next to him again. Then he says, "Well, I just can't decide. I'll think it over and come back."

The woman looks at both of us. And I can tell she suspects something. Then she shrugs and says, "Alright, then," and walks back to her place in front of the cash register.

We walk to a nearby park to split the goods. Sit at the picnic table stuffing our faces.

"That woman's stupid," Sawyer says, biting a MoonPie in half.

"She ain't."

"We come in there all the time and never buy nothing."

"She ain't stupid. She just don't care."

When we are finished, I take half the leftovers and give the other half to Sawyer. Then we walk the rest of the way home. When we get to his driveway, I wave goodbye. I live about a half mile down the highway from Sawyer. I could get home quicker if I cut through the woods, but I ain't got a mind to fool with briars and brambles and all that.

"See you tomorrow," Sawyer says, and I walk the road to our old house on the hill, thinking the whole time that maybe, just maybe, you are home waiting for me.

3

You need to come home. Your brother up here acting a fool. Says he owns this house.

Our house.

Says you ain't coming back. And since you ain't coming back, the house belongs to him. I try to tell him, but Momma tells me to be quiet and go inside. I am *not* a scared little boy anymore. But I go inside. I listen through the door, watching them both through the peephole.

Your brother looks like you. I pretend for a second he is. Tall and rangy, with knobby elbows and shoulders, deep-set eyes that carry fire right on the surface at all times. Watching him, I pretend you and Momma is having one of your talks in the yard. But his likeness isn't exact. More like a copy, but one that didn't come out right. You wear your brown hair cut short, but Wyatt's is all over the place and down around his shoulders. And even though he is bone skinny everywhere else, he has a pooch of fat on his stomach so big it looks like he is hiding a bowling ball under his shirt.

Wyatt waves a yellow folder, and I glimpse a stack of papers inside. He keeps shoving the folder toward Momma. "Lily, this place never belonged to him. Was never in Pa's will. Look right here, Lily. Never in the will."

Momma puts her hands on her hips and starts back toward the house. That's when your brother grabs her by the wrist. She spins, her brown hair fanning out. She looks stunned. Like *how dare you touch me*. And I am stunned too.

"Get your hands off me, Wyatt," she says.

But he don't let go.

"Look at this place, Lily," he says. "I stood by for a long time and done nothing, and you know why? Because I felt bad for you and Walker. I did, Lily. I felt *sorry* for you, but I can't no more. Look what Hank done to this place. Pa put everything he had into this farm, and look at it. Look at it!"

I look around. Crusty wallpaper hangs in curtains from the wall, shredded from the time you took a knife to it for no good reason at all. There is a red Igloo cooler on the counter, filled with ice and bologna and sandwich bread and ketchup and other things like that. We keep it there because the fridge stopped working, and you told Momma you would get the money to fix it, but you never did. So, every other day, Momma spends money on ice, just so we have a little food to eat. At least she *used* to before you took the truck and didn't come back.

Our floors sag. There's spots you can't step on unless you want your foot to crash through into the basement. And I don't know why, but there is a big wet spot in my room that never dries up. There are mushrooms growing on my walls and behind the toilet.

I know this place is a mess.

I *know* it.

But hearing him talk bad about it . . . talk bad about *you* . . . it gets my guts red hot. I grab my old BB gun leaning against the wall, the one you use to chase coons off the burn pile, and run out on the front porch. I point it at him. "Let her loose, Uncle."

Wyatt laughs, showing me his little nubbin teeth. "What do you plan to do with that peashooter, Walker?"

"I got good aim. I'll pop you in the eye."

He thinks about it for a minute. Then he turns her loose.

Turns out, Momma don't need my help. As soon as he lets go of her wrist, she wheels around and punches him right in the nose. Your brother yelps and staggers back. Momma comes at him again, but he hurries out of the way. He snatches up his yellow folder and points at it. "I'm coming for what's mine, Lily. Pa would roll in his grave to see this farm come to ruin. I don't aim to let that happen."

"Get out of here," Momma says.

"I'll have this drawn up legal. Get the law involved. They'll escort you out of here faster'n you can blink. Believe me, Lily. I got friends in the sheriff's office. I got friends everywhere."

"I *said* get out of here," Momma says.

And I wish you were here right now. Because I know Wyatt is scared of you. I know you wouldn't even have to raise a hand to scare him out of here. Then I think, if he's scared of you, then he is probably scared of me. I chuck the BB gun on the ground and come off the porch. I march straight toward him, and I can see him cower in front of me, and I won't lie, it feels good. I get so close to him, I can smell his Old Spice aftershave, same kind you wear.

"Momma said leave," I tell him.

He glares at me. He looks me up and down.

I ain't the small boy he used to pin down in the yard and thump in the chest with one knuckle over and over calling it *Chinese Water Torture*. I ain't the boy he used to try out wrasslin' moves on, slamming me one time into a pile of old bricks behind the barn.

No.

I'm grown now. Thick through the trunk, legs and arms like yours before the drugs wore you down. A linebacker.

Wyatt don't want none of this.

After a long pause, he backs away. "Fine," he says. "If you want to be like that."

He gives a little bow. Spins on his bootheel, and saunters back to his truck. "We'll see you soon, Lily," he calls. Then, toward me, "Walker. Be good."

Momma grabs my arm and drags me back toward the house.

"What's wrong?" I ask.

"You ought not do that."

"Do what?"

"Provoke him."

"He can't talk to us that way."

Momma slams the screen door. Glass rattles. She walks into the kitchen and puts both hands on the bar. She takes a deep breath, and I can tell she is choosing her next words carefully. After a minute, she picks up her cell phone and touches the screen like she is going to make a phone call. Blue light reflects on her narrow, tear-slick cheeks. Then she puts the phone face down on the bar. "Shit."

"What is it?"

"Out of minutes. On top of everything, out of minutes. Lord, can't even one thing swing our way?"

I agree with her. Seems like it can't. In my head, I think back to the Dollar General in between the school and our farm. They sell pre-paid phones, but they keep them locked behind glass. Too many folks already done what I am thinking about doing, so they lock them down.

"Walker," Momma says. Her eyes cut toward mine. Brown like coffee with no cream. "Don't be like those men."

"Like Uncle Wyatt?"

"Or Rufus. Or your daddy. Or any of his buddies."

I don't know what she means. "What's wrong with Daddy?"

"They're backward. Backward men."

I sit down on our old country farm-print couch, the one Pa left us when he died. Where Memaw sat all those years, her knitting needles clacking together as she spun together afghans easy as a spider.

What does Momma mean, "backward men"? I wish I could ask you. Are you backward, Daddy? Going the wrong way? If you are, then I am for sure backward too.

After a while, Momma starts going through cabinets. "You hungry?"

I nod. I am always hungry, seems like.

"You want mac and cheese with little hot dogs cut up in it?"

"My favorite."

She grabs a box of mac and cheese from the cupboard. And I see it's the last one. There's some ramen noodles up there. A packet of chili seasoning. Nothing else. She opens the red Igloo cooler on the bar, and I listen to her rummaging. She puts a half-eaten package of bologna on the bar. A carton of eggs. A gallon of milk. Three or four cheese slices and a package of Wonder Bread with nothing but the heels left.

Then she bursts into tears.

You would be proud of how I jump up and run to her. If there's one thing you taught me, it's nobody makes Momma cry and gets away with it. Right now, I feel a deep hatred for Uncle Wyatt bubble up in my stomach. I wish I'd shot him with that BB gun. Wish I'd knocked his teeth out when he was standing in front of me.

But when I ask Momma what is wrong, she doesn't say *Uncle Wyatt*.

She says, "Baby, I don't got any hot dogs for you."

"It's okay, Momma."

But she cries harder. "I don't got any money. I don't got a truck to go get a job. And my phone ain't got any minutes left."

She sits down at the kitchen table, and I realize something.

She is crying because of you. Because you left and didn't come back. Because our life is the way it is because you made it this way. So I guess when you said *don't nobody make Momma cry*, you meant, except you. *Nobody except you.*

I put my hand on her shoulder. Feel it shake and heave with her tears. "I don't care about hot dogs, Momma."

She laughs and cries at the same time.

"I'm going to find Daddy," I say. "I'm going to find him and make this right."

She gives me a cold stare through her tears. "And how do you plan to do that?"

"Could be some of his friends know where he is. What about Lukas Fisher?"

Momma grabs my chin, her fingers stained yellow from cigarettes. Hurts a little, but I don't show it. She pulls me close and puts more meanness in her voice than I ever heard in my life from her. "Don't you ever, *ever* go around your daddy's friends asking about where he is."

"Momma . . ."

"And don't *ever* go around Lukas for any reason ever. Do you hear me?"

"I hear you, Momma! I hear you!"

She shakes my whole face with her finger and thumb on my chin. "No. You have to promise me, Walker. Promise me right now. You will *never* go asking *anybody* after your daddy."

"Okay," I gasp. "I promise!" She turns me loose, and I rub the soreness out of my jaw, knowing right away that no matter what I *told* her, I am going to do whatever it takes to find you, even if that means talking to Lukas Fisher. "Jesus, Momma. What's so bad about Daddy and his friends, anyway?"

Momma dries her tears with her shirt, but more keep coming. She gets up and walks to the kitchen sink for a towel, which she gets wet. She wipes her whole face until her cheeks are red.

"What's so bad about his friends?" I ask again.

"They got anger in them," she says.

"Anger?"

"So much they can't feel nothing else."

"And Daddy too?"

She thinks hard on that question. Then says, "Sometimes, Walker. Sometimes."

4

On Wednesdays, I go see Mr. Raines, the school guidance counselor, because I punched Paton Roper in his stomach on the first day of school. You remember that? That was right before you disappeared. You remember he made fun of me because I had on these old Nike shoes we got from the donation bin at church, but it happened they were *his* old Nike shoes, so he had to go on and make sure everybody knew.

It's so stupid to me.

But I couldn't help but feel the anger churn inside.

Listening to him run his mouth, I remembered riding with you one time to Little Rock. You drove up there to sell a miter saw from Pa's garage you didn't need anymore. Met some man at a gas station off I-40, and he gave you a few hundred for the saw. You got back in the car with a grin.

I had a feeling I knew why. You were excited. You had a secret.

I needed new cleats for football, and I didn't tell you this back then, but I thought you were about to buy them with that money. Why else would you make me ride with you?

"Where we going?" I asked you.

You got back on the interstate. Got off at the next exit, still in Little Rock. I knew there were big shoe stores in Little Rock. The kind that sold the same kind of cleats NFL players wore on television.

"Someplace special," you said in an offhand way, like you were hiding something. And I thought I knew your secret. You were about to try and surprise me. You slowed the car. Hit the blinker, the sound like a foot tapping. I looked around. A sign on the building outside said *Smokies*. The *O* was painted to look like an eight ball. *Could be*, I thought. *Could be some kind of shoe store.*

"Wait out here for a while, Walker," you said.

And I did. Holding on to hope but my heart sinking the whole time.

I waited on you for two hours.

I was about to go inside when you fell backward through the entrance. You popped to your feet, fists already raised, and this big bald boy came tumbling through the glass double doors after you. I watched you tussle with him through the window until finally, you dipped away from a clumsy blow, dropped low, and punched him square under the chin.

When he hit the ground, you got in the truck in a hurry, cranked the key, and burned rubber on your way out of the parking lot.

"Why'd you do that?" I asked you.

And you said, and this is the part I really remember, "Walker, some folk won't know who you are until you tell 'em. Sometimes you gotta tell 'em with your fists."

So I told Paton who I was.

One punch, and he hit his knees.

One punch, and he cried right in front of everybody.

Stupid sheriff's boy.

After that, they suspended me for three days. They started making me come see Mr. Raines every Wednesday to talk about what he calls my "anger issues." And worst of all—a week ago, Mr. Raines changed what time we meet, so now they take me out halfway through English class. It's not that I *like* Mrs. Redman. But I like pretending to sleep at my desk so I can watch Chloe Ennis write in her creative writing notebook and pretend I've got a chance of ever being friends with her.

I like the way she talks. She's got no accent. And when she opens her zipper binder, I can't believe how nice she keeps things. Little tabs labeling every compartment. One just for paper clips. Six or seven pens all in a row. She has dividers separating loose-leaf paper, and all those are labeled too. One says *English*. Another says *science*.

One for each class. That is better than my system, which is to shove everything into my backpack until it gets crunched into nothing.

So when I walk into Mr. Raines's office, I'm not in the best mood already. Mr. Raines is a tall fella. Could be strong if he had any kind of hardness inside him. But he always asks me how I'm feeling, and I don't know what to tell him.

That's the first thing he says when I sit down.

"How are we feeling, Walker?"

"Fine."

"Fine?"

He looks at me through his glasses. You said to always look a man in his eyes, so I do. Because I want to show him I am strong like you. A lot of times, when you look someone in the eyes, they will look away. Not Mr. Raines. So even though there ain't a lick of hardness in him, he's got some kind of strength I don't know about hidden in there somewhere.

"I'm good, I swear," I say.

"Have you been writing in your journal like I asked?"

Last time we met, he said, "It's okay to be angry, but you have to express it in a healthy way." He gave me a leather-bound notebook and said, "I want you to write your thoughts in this."

I have the notebook in my backpack. But I look right at him and say, "No. I ain't keeping no diary."

"Why not?"

Mr. Raines's room is about as boring as a room can be. There's bookshelves behind him. Certificates from where he graduated school. There's even a picture of him shaking hands with an old president, and I'm not sure which one, but I think he was from Arkansas.

"I don't like it," I say.

"Why not?"

"I don't like writing big, long things. It's boring."

"You could try poetry? Poetry can be short."

I scowl at him. Of all the stupid things he could say to me. "Poems are for girls."

Mr. Raines shrugs. "No. Not really. A lot of men write wonderful poetry. But even if it were only women, would that really be a problem? Are you saying they can do something you can't?"

"No. Ain't saying that."

"I'm just saying, a poem might be easier. Just a few lines. It doesn't even have to rhyme. It just has to be honest. Sometimes, being honest can be a big help, even if it's just to yourself. Nobody ever has to read what you write. Not even me."

"Just say for one second I did this, and I'm not saying I am *going* to, but just pretend for one second I did—you won't try and read it?"

Mr. Raines raises his hand. It shakes in the air. Like a tremble. Like the way Memaw trembled so bad in the years before she died. The closer I watch him, the more I notice it. Mr. Raines shakes like an old person. It's like he can't never sit completely still.

"I promise I won't read it," he says. "But you know something kinda cool? If you *do* decide to show somebody, they might read it and say, 'I know exactly how this feels,' and knowing you aren't alone can be a really big help, you know? You can help them, and that can help you too, just by knowing you have both felt the same things."

I look at him for a long time. Finally, I say, "You made that up."

He gives me a little kind smile that says he feels sorry for me. "Give it a try," he says. "You might be surprised."

Coach lines us up for a little Oklahoma Drill during football practice. You would love it. All these boys slamming into each other. Throwing each other around. Figuring out who's strong and who ain't.

Sawyer stands next to me. "How was Mr. Raines?" he asks.

"Wants me to write poems."

Coach Widner hollers my name. My turn. I walk to the center of the circle and lay down in the grass, wondering who he'll pick for me to go against. I won't lie, I am hoping for Paton. Because when I leave Mr. Raines's office on Wednesdays, I can't help but remember why I'm there in the first place. Why I got to answer ten thousand questions about my *feelings*. Why I got to write in a journal. And why now, I *guess*, I got to think about writing poems too.

"Sawyer Metcalf," Coach Widner yells. "You're up."

And that's almost as good. Sawyer is the only boy on this team even close to being able to go against me in an Oklahoma Drill.

"Poetry is for girls," Sawyer says, laying down in the grass across from me. Our helmets a few feet apart.

"Shut up," I tell him.

Coach Widner blows the whistle. I jerk to my feet and spin. Sawyer is already hurtling toward me. I drop my shoulder. Our facemasks collide, and I'm so close to him, I can see little bubbles of sweat shake free from the tip of his nose. So close I can smell Doritos on his breath. We tangle there in the grass. The other boys whooping and hollering. Grunting and fighting. Until finally, I twist him sideways, and we land face-to-face on the grass.

"Ain't for girls if I do it," I say.

Sawyer spits out his mouthpiece laughing.

5

We walk the same way we always walk after school, but I have something else on my mind. I've been thinking about you and about Lukas Fisher. I think about Blackwater, the town right across the county line where folks go to get their liquor since we live in a dry county. As best I can tell, that is the source of most of your cutting up. You and Rufus, and Lukas, went there to drink almost every night of the week. And I've never been there, but if I had to guess, that photo you sent Momma the night you disappeared was probably taken in one of the bars there.

When we reach a Y in the road, I say, "Sawyer, you go on home. I'm going this way."

He gives me a look like *what the hell*, and says, "Where are you going?"

"Going to Blackwater."

"To the bars?"

"Yep."

I start walking. He follows beside me. I half expected that.

"What for?"

"Going to see about my daddy and yours. They was there all the time. Maybe somebody knows something."

"You think that's a good idea?"

"What are you? Afraid?"

Sawyer looks offended. "No," he says. "Let's go, then."

We walk along the highway in silence until we pass a small sign that says *Conway County*. Pressed right against the county line is a strip of buildings, all connected like the front street in the Western movies you and Pa used to watch. Every building is a different bar. And even though it is late afternoon, there are still cars parked in the parking lot. I've never been here before, but all the boys at school act like they come here on the weekends, show fake ID, buy booze or drink in one of the bars.

And maybe they do.

"Which one they go to?" Sawyer says.

"Hell, they probably went to all of them," I say.

I figure I'll hit them one at a time. I start toward the farthest to the right. Sawyer grabs my arm. "I got a shit feeling about this. Even if they was here, nobody gonna tell us nothing."

"Why not?"

He shakes his head. "Nobody talks, Walker. That's rule number one. Nobody God damn talks. And you know what else? What if we walk in there, and they are inside on a month-long bender. What then?"

"Then we bring them home?"

"What if they don't want to come?"

I sigh. "The truck ain't here, Sawyer. Come on."

I go inside the first bar. A sign outside says *Mike's Spot*. The whole place looks like it's been carved from the inside of an old tree. Right away, I know this is where the photo had been taken. A neon sign hangs on the wall, dim now but glowing bright in that photo. Says *Coors*, just like in the photo of you.

A man comes from the back, leans across the bar, and glares at me, yellow pit stains soaking through his white T-shirt. "How old are you?"

"Fifteen," I say.

"Twenty-one," Sawyer says at the same time.

"Out," the man says, pointing at the door.

I know I don't have long to protest, so I say it straight up. "We ain't here to drink. We're lookin' for our dads."

The man relaxes a little. "Who are your dads?"

"Hank Lauderdale," I say.

"And Rufus Metcalf," Sawyer adds.

"I heard they was missing," the man says. He comes around the bar and stands in front of us, muscled arms crossed across his fat belly.

"They were here the last time anybody saw them," I say.

"They were?"

"I need to find them real bad."

"You need to go to the police. I can't help you. Now, run off." He starts toward the back room, itching his ass with one hand.

I hurry to catch up with him. "Now, hold on a second."

He stops. I look at Sawyer, who just blinks at me.

"Did you see him? Do you know where I can find him?"

He licks his lips, his tongue slimy like a slug. "Y'uns need to get out of here."

He starts to walk away, but I grab his wrist, jerk him toward me. He blows up, like he might start throwing fists, and I know just by looking at him he's fooled around with drunks and meth addicts enough to know his way around a fight.

"You know something," I say.

Sawyer steps closer to me. We are only fifteen, but we are a big fifteen.

The man's eyes dart back and forth between us. "Y'uns need to leave," he says again, slowly this time, "before I call the law on you." He jerks his hand free from my grasp. "Touch me again, I might come unglued."

He walks behind the bar, hovers his hand over the phone. I know he knows something. And the fact that I know, and he won't tell me, got all my insides twisted up. I tighten a fist at my side and think I might could beat it out of him. He has thick arms, but he is soft in the middle. *One punch*, I think. He'd go down like Paton did.

Then what?

Would he tell me then?

Probably not.

Sawyer must know what I am thinking. He puts a hand on my shoulder and shakes his head. "Come on," he whispers.

I look at the man. He picks up the phone, makes like he is going to dial.

"If we don't find them, we might could starve to death," I say.

"Might could end up homeless. We'll leave, but it's real important. I hope you know that."

The man blinks at us. Sawyer tugs my arm, and we go outside.

Sawyer lifts a couple soda bottles from a gas station across the street. We sit on the curb drinking them.

"This is some shit," I say.

"Mhm."

I finish off that soda and chuck the empty bottle into the woods. Sawyer done the same. I look back at the bars one last time, thinking maybe I ought to go inside and try again. Just then, the door to Mike's Spot opens, and the big-armed man steps outside. He looks around for a second, sees us, then walks straight up.

"You ain't heard shit from me," he says.

"Huh?" I say.

"Anyone asks, you heard nothing from me."

I still ain't sure what he means, so I just say, "Oh."

"I mean *nothing*, y'uns was never here."

Sawyer elbows me. "We were never here," he says. "Got it."

"Hank and Rufus was up here anytime there was a game, anytime they had money, anytime they had nothing else to do. They was rowdy, but they never caused me no trouble. I heard they was selling dope or crank or both or something from some boys Lukas was running with when he weren't with your dads. Heard a deal gone bad. Heard some folks was really angry. Could be, I thought, them three went into hiding, trying to save they skin. But then I heard something else . . ."

Hearing this is like getting an inside look into your world. You sell drugs?

I guess I shouldn't be surprised, how often you came home high. But I am.

The big guy looks around nervously as if somebody might hear him. He runs a hand through his hair. "Aw, hell. I shouldn't be saying this."

I look straight at him. Honesty worked last time, so I try again. "Please. I need to know."

He swallows. "I reckoned all three maybe was in hiding, then Lukas showed up here the other night. Bought a round of drinks for the whole bar, and we had the Cowboys game on, so the place was full. I asked him about Hank. About Rufus. He said, and I remember this clear as crystal, he said, *Don't worry, they around.*" He pauses, wipes sweat off his brow. A car pulls into the parking lot, and he watches it drive by. "If I was looking for them, there's only one place I would start."

We don't say nothing.

"That's with Lukas Fisher," he says. "Lukas Fisher . . . and that's God's truth."

6

We got a road game in Manning, taking on the Goblins. Before we get on the bus, Coach Widner has us sit in the bleachers in the gymnasium. He stands right on the orange-and-blue War Eagle on the center of the floor and tells us to shut our mouths.

"This is a lousy football team," he says.

That gets our attention since we won pretty easy last week.

"You feel mighty because you whooped on Steelville," he says, his fists on his hips. "Feel like you're *somebody* now, don't you? Well, one game don't mean a thing. You are still the same football program you were when I got here. Ten straight losing seasons. And you'll be that same team . . . until you go out on that field and change it."

The silence is heavy in the room. I can feel it tense on my shoulders.

"That starts tonight. And it starts in here." He points to his temple. "Starts right now. Starts with *focus*. I don't want to hear one sound on the drive to Manning. Because you ain't got time to talk. You only got time to focus. Our goals are in order, men. First winning season in ten years. Make the playoffs. And from there . . . we can go as far as you want to drive this thing."

He stares at us for a long moment. Then he blows his whistle and barks, "Load up."

I sit by Sawyer on the drive. Coach Widner drives the bus, both hands on the wheel, a Dum-Dum sucker tucked between his teeth and cheek.

"Let's go, men," he hollers, as he cranks the engine.

We buzz through the bendy roads of Northern Arkansas. Sometimes the trees fall away, and we can see the valley below, one block of trees, one block of cow land. Like the quilts Memaw used to make when she was alive.

"Do you know where Lukas Fisher lives?" I ask Sawyer.

He sucks his teeth, looks uncomfortable. "Why are you asking me this?"

"That's not a 'no.'"

"Why do you want to know?"

"You know why."

"You ever stop and think our daddies don't want to be found?" Could be.

Until Sawyer said it right then, I hadn't even thought about it. There's a chance you left us. You got in your truck, and you left us in the squalor of Pa's old farm. Left us to ruin. To die in these mountains.

I put my head back on the seat. Whole bus shakes and bounces on the uneven roads. "Damn," I whisper.

I look at Sawyer sideways. He looks a little sad. Then he gives me his crooked, missing-tooth smile and says, "Hey, Walker, tell me about that girl from your English class."

And I can't help it. I smile right back. Thinking of Chloe Ennis makes me smile even when I don't feel like smiling. "She don't know me."

"Small school. Everybody know everybody."

"Maybe it's a good thing she don't know me."

"Why?"

I'm not sure how to answer him. I don't want her to know I live in a run-down farmhouse on the edge of the county. I don't want her to know I punched Paton Roper before school. Don't want her to know I keep a secret journal. Don't want her to think less of me. I pick my words carefully, and hearing them come out of my mouth feels like weight landing on my chest. "I want her to think I'm a good person."

Sawyer frowns a little. Nods like he understands. He leans his head against the bus window, leaving a smear in the condensation.

"Well, you should talk to her anyway."

I don't say anything. We drive on through the mountains, and I try to point my brain at better thoughts. Like football games against the Manning Goblins. Like finding you. Figuring out it was all a mistake, and you wanted to be here all along. Only some small thing is keeping you back. If I can talk to Lukas, ask him where you are, and I can go there and find you, everything will go back to the way it's supposed to be.

Because if I was missing . . . you would look for me.

You would, right?

You'd look for me?

I know you would.

We win 35–3. You aren't there. I knew you wouldn't be. But still, I scanned the bleachers before the game. I let myself think, *Maybe Daddy ran off to Manning, and he's here, and he knows I'm playing tonight, and he'll be in the crowd watching.*

But no.

Of course not.

Just so you know, by the end of the game, I had eleven tackles. Six solo. Three for loss. Sawyer had six tackles. Three solo. Two for loss, plus an interception and a forced fumble. Sawyer is really fast. Maybe I'm a little stronger than he is, but he makes up for it by being quicker than bullshit.

You'd have been proud.

You *and* Rufus.

If you'd been there.

7

I walk to Sawyer's house when I wake up. Think about you. Think about poems and Mr. Raines. Think about football. Replay one tackle I had last night in my mind over and over. The offensive line opened like a door, and I blindsided their lefty quarterback. I wonder what you'd have said after the game. I know you'd have been proud.

I knock on Sawyer's door. He isn't awake, so I go inside. His momma, Aunt Maybelle, is asleep on the couch, about twenty beer cans piled up on the floor around her, a cigarette still burning across the top of one of them, ash dripping into the opening. I don't wake her. I walk through the kitchen, past the dishes in the sink, the gnats hovering over the trash can, a stack of dirty magazines on the kitchen table, crammed between old newspapers, soda cans, and plates of half-eaten food turning white and puffy with age.

"Wake up," I say, standing in Sawyer's doorway.

He sits up and rubs his eyes, his blond hair all over the place. "What time is it?"

"Eight."

He collapses back into bed, pulls his sleeping bag over his head. "Fuck off, Walker."

"I need you to tell me where Lukas lives."

Sawyer groans. But I don't budge.

"It is too early for this shit," he says.

"Sawyer, come on."

He sits up again. Yawns big, showing he is missing more than just his front tooth. "Lukas is perma-stoned. About half-crazy. What makes you think finding him will help, even if he does know something?"

"You could be right, but what else can I do?"

"Don't waste your time foolin' with that old cuss."

"What if it do help? Don't you want to find your dad?"

Sawyer puts his feet on the floor. "Depends on how he acts when he gets here."

"The hell does that mean?"

Sawyer rolls his eyes. Rubs sleep out of them. "Course I want to find him, Walker. It's just something happened with Lukas you don't know about."

I cross the room, pretend I don't see the dirty underwear on the floor, and sit down on the edge of his bed. "Sawyer," I say. "If we don't find my dad, we going to lose our house. I'll have to move away. I don't know where. Maybe not even in Arkansas anymore. We might even be all the way homeless."

Sawyer rolls over in bed, pulling his sleeping bag over his shoulder. He doesn't say anything for a long time. So long, I'm about to turn around and holler at him. Then he peeps at me over his shoulder.

"Thing is, he come up here a few weeks ago, like maybe a week before our dads run off, waving a gun around. Daddy went out on the front porch, and I saw Lukas point it at him. Daddy snatched it out of his hand and clubbed him over the head with it. Then told him to get out of here. I saw it all through the window. Momma went out there too, and she was yelling at Lukas, 'What is wrong with you? Coming here with a gun? In front of Sawyer? Are you crazy?'"

"So what?"

"So he's no good, Walker. And he stirs shit up. Bad emotions. 'Cause after he was gone, Momma really laid into Daddy. Started yelling and screaming. And you know him. He weren't putting up with that. Slapped her right in the face. Gun still in the other hand. Five. Six. Seven times. Until she was begging him to stop. I run out the house and pulled him off her. Gut checked him one time. Hard as I could. Was like punching a brick wall. So then he whooped me too."

"Damn." It's funny 'cause I always thought Rufus was a little better than you. At least in terms of not flying off the handle. He had a cool way about him. Slow and deliberate. Like you couldn't shake him. I guess it shows you never can tell what happens when ain't nobody around to judge. I feel awkward. I want to change the subject. So I say, "Where's that gun now?"

"Daddy's room."

"So grab it and we can go shoot."

Aunt Maybelle doesn't stir when we walk past her. She looks dead, to tell you the truth. Like a skeleton with some meat still on it. Her short brown hair is greasy and plastered to her forehead. The tattoos on both her shoulders are so faded they look like puddles of spilled ink, and her lips are suctioned tight into her toothless mouth, like a woman three times her age.

We walk to the back room, and Sawyer pulls the gun out of the closet. He pops out the magazine. Fully loaded. Then he clicks on the safety and sticks the gun in his waistband. Hides it under his War Eagles sweatshirt.

Good thing too.

On the way out, Maybelle is sitting up in the recliner. She is shaking a lot like Mr. Raines shakes. Trembles all over her body. She says, "God. Jesus," while holding herself in a hug. Then she sees us. "What are you up to, baby?"

"Just going outside," Sawyer says. "Go back to sleep."

"Done slept enough. Why you ain't come over here and hug your momma?"

Sawyer's shoulders tighten, but he takes a few small steps toward her. She stands, wobbles, then moves toward him. She puts her arms around his shoulders and her withered mouth against his cheek. "I been dreaming, Sawyer," she whispers, her voice somehow wet and raspy at the same time.

"Dreaming?" he asks.

"About what we'll do with ourselves once we got money. Once we ain't poor and living in this hellhole of a trailer." She looks at me when she says this.

"We ain't never getting money, Momma."

She turns him loose. She laughs, showing me her gums, looking like a wicked witch from some old movie. "Yes, we are, Sawyer. We gonna come into some money real soon, I promise you. Real, real soon."

She's always saying stuff like this. Especially when she's out of her mind on whatever drugs she filled her body with.

"Okay, Momma," Sawyer says. He pushes past her.

"I'll see you later, Aunt Maybelle," I say, as we walk through the screen door.

"Tell my sister I said hello," she says, sitting back down, picking up a glass pipe and a lighter. "Tell her to come see me some time."

"I will." I shut the door, and we hurry down the steps. Sawyer stops at the bottom and exhales.

"You ever feel like something is crushing you?" he says. "Like something is sitting on your chest and crushing you. And if you cain't get out from under it, you gonna die?"

"I don't know," I say. "Maybe."

He starts walking toward the woods. "Yeah, never mind," he says. "Let's go."

I grab a trash bag full of soda cans from under the front deck and sling it over my shoulder. We walk behind Sawyer's trailer, deep into the woods that connect our properties. I don't really want to shoot anything, but I know Sawyer is crazy about guns. I think maybe if I can get him doing something he loves, he might tell me what he knows about Lukas at the same time.

When we get far enough away, I balance the soda cans on a log.

"This is a Colt 1911, single-action, semi-automatic, with eight .45 rounds," Sawyer says, lining up the gun for a shot. Sawyer likes to know about guns. He's got magazines in his room about them. Survival magazines about how to live if you ever got lost in the wilderness or if the world ever ended.

Blam!

The sound makes my ears ring. One can bounces from the log, falling to the ground with a rattle.

"Drop a man in one shot," Sawyer says.

Blam!

Another can pops into the air, then falls to the ground with a clunk. My ears ring even more. I want to clap my hands over them, but I don't want Sawyer to think I am chicken. Truth is, I never shot a gun besides my BB gun before.

"Let me take the gun with me," I say.

"With you?" Sawyer glances at me sideways.

"When I talk with Lukas."

Sawyer shakes his head. "No."

"Why not? You said he's no good."

"One thing about guns is sometimes they only make it worse. The best thing, Walker, is to just stay away from folks like Lukas altogether."

"Lukas was friends with our dads."

Sawyer doesn't say anything to this. He reels off another three shots, missing all three, then puts the gun in my palm.

"I know where he lives," he says. "But believe me when I say it won't help. At best, it's a waste of time. At worst . . ."

"What? What's the worst?"

"I don't want to think about it."

The gun is heavier than I expected. I lift it, close one eye, and put a can in my sight.

Blam!

One thing I learn then: A gun is heavy, but the trigger pulls easy. Almost too easy. There's no time to change your mind once it's started. That trigger goes down, and fire comes out, and there's no stopping it. Once it goes, it goes for good.

The can spins backward off the log.

"Good shot," Sawyer says.

Bellwork
In the space below, write a funny memory from your childhood
_____

One Christmas there were no gifts and no tree. I was five, I think. I asked daddy everyday when we was getting a tree. One day he stood up and said TODAY. He fell down two times walking to the truck. I rode in the back and we went all the way to the city. He bought the biggest tree they had. But when we got home he couldn't get it together right. All the big pieces were on top. All the small pieces were on bottom. I laugh anytime I little remember that funny tree.

8

At lunch, Mr. Raines walks by my table, where me and Sawyer and some other football players are sitting. He leans over and puts both hands on the table and looks right at me. "How are we feeling today, Walker?" he says. And I swear to you, the whole table stops talking to look at me.

I feel my cheeks turn bright red. Like fire is underneath them. But I am strong like you, so I swallow it down. Bury it deep. I look back at him and say, "It was better before you got here."

That gets the boys laughing.

Mr. Raines laughs too. "You hate me, I get it!" Then he points at me, and I can see the little tremble in his finger. He's trying to act cool. Trying to make us like him. "Hey, you should write a poem about it."

When he leaves, Paton says, "Hey, Walker, is that what you been doing on Wednesdays when you go to his office? Writing poems? Or you been doing *something else*?"

I hate the way he says *something else*. His lips and tongue smacking between chewed-up ham sandwich. "What do you mean?"

"Ain't he a little"—he stops and whispers this next part— "squirrelly?"

"Squirrelly?" I say, because I have no clue what he means.

Paton leans closer. "You two writing poems together? Sounds *romantic*."

Another round of laughter. I should have stood up right then and punched him. But something stops me. Maybe it is because I know I'll get suspended again. And if that happens, I won't get to play football. Or maybe it's knowing I'd have to talk to Mr. Raines about it, knowing he'd ask me to explain exactly how I am feeling.

I glance at Sawyer. He takes over for me. "Shut up, Paton."

Paton shrugs, keeps running his mouth. You said sometimes you got to tell people who you are. I told Paton, but he still don't get it. I got this feeling I'm going to have to tell him again and again.

Sawyer reaches across the table and slaps the sandwich out of Paton's hand. The laughing stops. All our eyes are on Sawyer.

"Shut your mouth, or I'll shut it for you," Sawyer says.

Paton opens his mouth to say something else. Sawyer slaps him across the face. Hard enough the entire cafeteria falls silent. Kids turn in their seats to watch. Cell phones come out, recording. I crane around, sure a teacher will come barreling across the lunchroom to separate them. But none come. Paton rubs his cheek. His eyes smolder like coal, like he wishes he could kill Sawyer right there. And for a second, he looks strong. Like he has toughness in him. I might have believed it. But I know better.

Paton's mouth snaps closed.

He doesn't say another word during lunch.

9

I pass Chloe Ennis in the hall. She walks alone, her books tight against her chest. She wears a pair of ripped-up jeans and a man's flannel shirt. She doesn't look up when she passes me.

I think, *I oughta say something. I oughta walk beside her.*

I remember in old movies, sometimes boys would ask to carry a girl's books to class. But nobody does that anymore. How do you get to know somebody brand new? How do you talk to them without being weird? Without being a creep? How do you tell them you want to know them better? All this flashes through my mind in less time than it takes a center to snap a football.

Then she is gone. Around the corner. Out of sight. But not out of mind. Not my mind, anyway.

10

nvictus,'" Mr. Raines says, thumping a piece of paper on the desk, "is a poem written by a man."

There is an envelope on the corner of his desk. I don't think he means for me to see it. It is from Saint Mary's Hospital, the big one in the city. Same place Pa spent the last three weeks of his life before he finally died.

"What's that?" I say, mainly because I know it'll make him uncomfortable.

His eyes widen. He snatches the envelope and tucks it into one of the drawers of his desk. "Nothing," he says. There's a funny sound in his voice. Like he is forcing the words out.

"So I have to tell you everything, but you don't got to tell me nothing?"

Mr. Raines laughs a little. "It's a bill, Walker. One I'm going to have to get creative to figure out how to pay." He touches the paper in front of me. "Now, back on task. 'Invictus' is a poem written by a man."

"So what?"

"So you think poems are for girls. I'm showing you they are for everyone." He nudges the paper closer to me. "Why don't you read this out loud?"

I don't read too good out loud. I can read just fine in my head, but when I try to read out loud, especially in front of other people, the words get jumbled in my mouth. It's like I forget how to read at all. I got to read slow and sound out words like some kind of moron.

But Mr. Raines don't care. "Go on," he says.

I pick up the piece of paper. Think of you right then. Because I always do. You always sneak into my thoughts at weird times. Slowly, I read the poem out loud. "Out of the night that covers me . . . black as the pit . . . as the pit . . . from pole to pole . . ."

I stumble over every word, barely understanding any of it. When I finish, Mr. Raines leans back at his desk. He puts his hands behind his head and says, "Well, what'd you think?"

"I don't even understand one word."

"To me, it's about strength against adversity."

I glance down at the poem and read it again, this time to myself so I can follow it better. Mr. Raines keeps talking.

"This was written in 1875 by William Ernest Henley," he says. "He knew a little bit about suffering because he had tuberculosis."

I stare up from the paper at him.

"It's a disease. What does the poem mean to you?"

I put the paper back on his desk. "Means nothing to me."

"Do you know what the word *invictus* means?"

"Nope."

"Unconquerable." He says it like he thinks it might impress me. Like he thinks I like these kinds of words. I blink slowly at him. After a second, he laughs at himself. Shakes his head. "That got nothing, huh? Let me ask you this instead . . . what does strength mean to you?"

That makes me think of you again. Strongest person I know. Makes me wonder, *What exactly makes you so strong?*

"Being strong means making things happen how they ought to happen," I say.

Mr. Raines smiles. He leans forward, and I can tell he is really listening to what I have to say. That makes me feel like I want to say more, so I add, "It's fixing things when they go wrong. It's never needing help. It's doing it by yourself."

Mr. Raines nods while I'm speaking. "And who gets to decide how things ought to happen, which things need fixing?"

I cram the poem into my backpack. That is a good question, but I know the answer. I tell him, "Whoever is the strongest."

I have no clue.

Like Jesus?

Out of the night that covers me,
  Black as the pit from pole to pole,
I thank whatever gods may be
  For my unconquerable soul.

this makes me think of you.

In the fell clutch of circumstance
  I have not winced nor cried aloud.
Under the bludgeonings of chance
  My head is bloody, but unbowed.

Hell.

Beyond this place of wrath and tears
  Looms but the Horror of the shade,
And yet the menace of the years
  Finds and shall find me unafraid.

It makes me think of me.

It matters not how strait the gate,
  How charged with punishments the scroll,
I am the master of my fate,
  I am the captain of my soul.

Strong no matter what.

nobody never could tell you what to do.

11

We have a road game against Wood River. It's all a blur. I play good defense. Make lots of tackles, and I even get to run the football twice on offense. Coach Widner keeps saying I am "aggressive" and "mean" and he "*loved* that." After one tackle, he says to me, "A good linebacker *ought* to be a little mean."

I feel happy when he says that, but then I feel sad right after because I wish you were here to see it. I wish you were here so I could tell you about it after.

After the game, a 21–8 victory, the team hangs around the locker room looking at their phones and talking, waiting on Coach to say it's time to leave. I don't have a phone, so I just change clothes and sit there waiting on Sawyer to get out of the shower. I watch him walk across the locker room with a towel pinned around his waist. He gets halfway to me when Paton stands up and says, "Hey, Walker, they found your dad."

Paton turns his phone toward me, a video from a news station in Little Rock playing on the screen. I cannot tell if he is making fun of me or not.

"Shut the fuck up, Paton," Sawyer says, snatching the phone out of his hands. Paton tries to grab the phone, but Sawyer keeps it away from him. He sits beside me, and we stare down at the screen. I see police lights flashing. Cars parked along the muddy bank of a lake. They lift a truck from the water on iron cables attached to a crane. It spins in a slow circle, spewing old water from rolled-down windows.

And it is your truck.

Paton is right.

It is *your* truck.

I feel alone then. Like nobody else is in the room. Sawyer turns up the audio in time for me to hear the news lady say, *"Authorities fished the vehicle out of Lake Nimrod early this morning. There were no occupants inside, and its owner has yet to be identified."*

But everyone in that locker room knows it is your blue Dodge Ram, faded to gray and rust on the top, Arkansas Razorbacks sticker on the back glass. Everyone stands around quiet, watching us watch the video over and over, looking for any clue it wasn't your truck. That it is some other truck. That you ain't drove to Lake Nimrod, wherever that is, and put our only wheels in the bottom of the water.

"It's his," Sawyer says, so quiet only I can hear. "I know it's his."

Most of the time, we walk home after a game. Even when it's dark. But Coach Widner drives up in his big black Ford, Mississippi tags still on the back, and rolls down the window.

"Hop in," he says before we can even leave school property.

I don't want to ride with him, honestly, but I am feeling a little beat up. We get in the cab. His truck isn't like yours at all. Everything is new inside. Shiny. Lots of dials and knobs that glow in the dark. Truth is, I want to walk home. I want to tell Sawyer he *has* to tell me where Lukas Fisher lives now. Because now it's worse than our daddies being missing. They are missing and our truck is sunk in a lake.

We drive in silence for a while. Coach Widner clears his throat a few times like he wants to talk but keeps changing his mind. Finally he says, "You boys okay?"

"Fine, Coach," Sawyer says.

"Walker?" Coach Widner says.

"Fine," I say, without looking at him.

I don't feel fine. Not way down deep inside. Feel like a pond frozen over in the winter. Clean on top, but scummy down deep. But I know saying this would be a bad idea because Coach Widner might think I am weak. I want him to know I am as strong and mean as he is always saying I am during football games.

"I understand if you ain't," he says.

"Ain't what?" I say.

"Ain't fine. It's tough what's happening."

"We're fine," I say.

When we get to the road that leads to Sawyer's trailer, Sawyer taps Coach Widner on the shoulder. "Let me off here," he says.

"I can drive you up to the front door."

"No, just let me off at the end of the drive."

"You sure?"

"Yes, sir."

Coach Widner pulls into the driveway a little but stops and lets Sawyer climb out. Then Coach Widner backs onto the highway, changes gears, and drives the rest of the way to our farm. He doesn't ask if I want to be let out. He drives down our driveway like he owns the place. When we come out of the trees, I see two sheriff deputies parked in our yard. They are standing on the front porch knocking on the door. I know Momma won't open for any kind of law, but I also know she don't know about your truck.

"Stop here," I say.

Coach Widner does, and I jump out fast. I run through the yard. The deputies turn and see me. One of them isn't a deputy at all. It's the sheriff himself. Paton's daddy.

"Hey, son, hold up right there a minute," he says when he sees me coming.

I stop in the yard, tall grass tickling the back of my legs.

"My name's Sheriff Roper." He sticks the hat back on his head.

"I know you."

He rests his forearm on the gun on his hip, leaning to one side. He nods over his shoulder, a little dip of his big cowboy hat toward the house. "Can you fetch your momma? It's real important. We know she's in there."

And I know you'd be mad at me, but I open the door to the law anyway. I shoulder past Sheriff Roper and the other deputy, holler inside for Momma. She is sitting right on the couch, her eyes wide and scared. I look right at her. Try my best to use the tone you use when something is important. When you want me to stop and pay attention. Want me to know whatever it is you're saying to me is serious.

"Momma, come on," I say.

She stands and walks toward me. When she gets on the porch, Sheriff Roper looks down at me. "Son, why don't you wait inside?"

This is happening like in the movies. Where they give a woman bad news on her porch. But I refuse to believe that news is gonna be *Hank Lauderdale is dead*.

I refuse.

They found that truck in the water, but they didn't find you inside it.

I scowl at Sheriff Roper. "I can hear it."

Momma looks like a shell of the woman I know. Going through the motions. She looks like she might throw up. Looks like a ghost from a movie, one that appears in the top-floor window of some old house, with a look on its face that says *everything hurts*. I watch her eyes move from the sheriff to Coach Widner, where she pauses for too long, like they have a silent conversation together. Finally, she looks at me.

She comes closer and puts one soft hand on my cheek. And something about that reminds me of being small. Back when I thought Momma could kiss away scraped knees. I want to crawl into her arms. Cry into her neck.

But I know I can't.

You gotta be strong, boy, your voice says to me, filtering down through all my memories and into that moment as if you are standing right behind me.

"Why don't you head inside, baby," she whispers.

There is softness in her eyes. Softness like I never seen before. But I can't bring myself to go inside the house. Instead, I hop off the front porch and run into the woods. Momma calls after me, but I don't stop. I keep going, tree limbs slapping and tearing at my face, until I come out in the field behind Sawyer's trailer. I stand there a minute, steam puffing from my mouth. I touch a burning scratch across my cheek and my fingers come away red.

As I walk closer, I see a pair of deputies standing outside the trailer. It looks like they've already given their bad news. They lean against the back of their cruiser, one smoking a cigarette, the other hocking chewing tobacco into a green Mountain Dew bottle.

I sneak up on them. Hide at the edge of the trailer, down on one knee, ready to run if either of them turns and sees me. I listen to them speak. Low tones, like two bears growling at each other.

"You reckon they're dead?" one says.

"Most like."

Hearing that is like a punch in the stomach. I want to jump up then and tell them *no, my daddy is too strong to be dead. Too full of life. My daddy is so mean, he'd look death right in the face and tell it to go fuck itself.*

You aren't dead, Daddy.

I can't accept that. Not until I see for myself. Touch your cold skin with my fingers.

One of the deputies spits into the bottle, scraping it across his lips to clean off the extra tobacco juice. "Welp," he says, screwing on a bottle cap.

"Welp," the other says, smashing his cigarette out on the heel of his boot. "Guess some problems take care of themselves, don't they?"

The other officer laughs. "Looks like."

I watch them get back in the cruiser. Laughing and cutting up. Like they ain't just shattered an entire world. I watch them back out of Sawyer's driveway and disappear into the woods. I listen to their engine fade in the distance. Then I listen to the sound of crickets singing. A hoot owl asking questions. A distant loon crying in a way I know I never can.

12

Can't stop thinking about it. A problem taking care of itself? Is those deputies calling *you* a problem? I guess they got tired of coming out and talking you down on our front porch. Got tired of all the fighting. All the drugs. I guess when folks get tired of dealing with somebody, it ain't so bad if their truck turns up at the bottom of Lake Nimrod. Guess some folks figure you're better off dead than alive. More trouble than you're worth. And I guess if *you're* more trouble than you're worth, then so am I.

The team always meets at the school on Saturday to watch film. But I ain't going. I know all I'll do is think about how the me in that grainy footage still don't know your truck was at the bottom of Lake Nimrod.

Feel sorry for that poor fool.

Momma cries off and on all morning. Ain't nothing to eat, so I'm starving. That's one good thing about going to school. The booster club always feeds the team, so I get one good meal in my stomach no matter what else.

But not today.

Being with Momma is more important than football today.

I spend half the morning going through the cupboards, looking for something to eat. I find a box of Hamburger Helper tucked in the back of the cabinet, behind a box of salt. We ain't got any meat, and we ain't got milk or any of the other things it calls for on the box, but I cook it anyway. Just some noodles in some watery sauce. I give a bowl to Momma and sit down beside her.

"What are we going to do, Walker?" Momma asks me.

"He'll come back," I tell her. "He wouldn't leave us like this. You should eat them noodles. I can't remember last time I seen you eat."

"I eat, Walker," she says.

But I don't believe her. Even though my stomach is screaming like a stuck pig, I gave her most of the noodles. I know she done that kind of thing plenty of times for me. But I ain't letting it happen again. Not today. She takes a forkload into her mouth and chews. I dump the rest of my bowl into hers.

Around noon, your brother, Wyatt, turns up on the front porch. "Found his truck, did they?" Wyatt yells through the door. "He's dead, Lily. *Dead.*"

We watch him through the window. And there is real fear in Momma's eyes. Wyatt's boots thump up and down the porch. I start to go outside, to run him off like I done before, but Momma grabs my arm. She points, and I see it. A gun stuck in his belt.

What a coward.

One thing I learned about guns. They make weak men feel like they are strong.

"Lily, get your ass out here so we can talk," he says. One finger taps the butt of the pistol. "I only want to talk to ya. Is that so hard?"

His face darkens the window, his hands cupped around his eyes. We drop low, hoping he can't see us. Then he vanishes. He wiggles the doorknob, but it is locked. I listen to his boots thump, thump, thump across our wooden porch. He talks to himself. Curses at us. Curses at you. Says you ruined this whole farm. Destroyed the house that meant so much to Pa. Says he is going to get it all drawn up legal. Tells us to go ahead and leave now. Make things easier on ourselves.

Easier.

Can you believe he said that? Ain't nothing easy about any of this.

If we're out of the house, where do we go?

The whole time he is here, I wish you would show up at the end of the drive. Stand there and stare at him like a cowboy in the movies.

Or maybe walk out of the woods and holler his name. I can imagine him freezing in place. Scared to death because you ain't dead. And Wyatt likes to pretend he's strong like you. But he ain't. Not even close.

After a long time, he gets in his truck, the engine roaring like a monster, and leaves.

When he is gone, I know I don't have a choice. I can't wait any longer. I have to find you right away. I grab my backpack and walk through the woods and knock on Sawyer's door, hoping he can tell me where to find Lukas Fisher, but nobody answers.

Then I remember Sawyer probably went to school to watch film.

When I get back to my place, Coach Widner's truck is in the driveway. I stare at the Mississippi tags, thinking, *You don't belong here. Go back where you belong.* Why he isn't at school like Sawyer? He isn't in his truck, so I creep through the yard. I make my way to the same window Wyatt peered through just a little earlier.

I see Coach Widner sitting on our old farm-print couch next to Momma. She cries hard into her hands, and he rubs little circles on her back.

I can't hear them.

I listen hard, but their voices are like water in a creek bed. Murmurs.

Then Momma looks up at him. Tears all over her face. Like a moment in a movie or television show, where you know before it happens what comes next. Coach Widner's hand moves to her shoulder. Then up her neck. Then onto her cheek. His brown skin is stark against hers. I keep expecting her to move away. To slap his hand down. But she doesn't. She looks up at him and closes her eyes.

I hurry to the front door and throw it open. Coach Widner shoots to his feet.

"Hey, Walker," he says, stumbling with his words a little. "Jesus, you scared the hell out of me. I just come up here to check on you. See if you were coming to film study."

I can't find any words.

I ball my fists. They shake at my sides. I think, *If I stand here one more second, I am going to punch this man right in his fat stomach.*

Lord, I should do it.

Instead, I give them the meanest look I got and turn away. I hurry back out the door and into the woods. This time, I don't go toward Sawyer's trailer. Instead, I cut north, deeper into the thicket. Where there ain't nobody, and I know nobody can find me. Once I know I am alone, I throw my backpack on the ground and collapse in the tangled roots of an old tree. I lean my head back against its trunk and look up at the golden sun shimmering through green leaves.

Mr. Raines said writing *poems* can help. Said being *honest* can make it better. He's wrong. Nothing can make it better. But there is too much mixed up inside my head. I have to do something or it is going to explode out of me. I grab my notebook and a pen from my backpack. I yank off the cap with my teeth and touch the nib to the page. A little black spot of ink leaks out. I stare at it for a long time, wondering how I am supposed to be honest about any of this.

Then I write.

my blood is on fire
because I'm not strong
because if I was
I would change everything
money in our pocket
food in our fridge
a truck that can go

I'd buy new sneakers
I'd buy new cleats
not the kind you get in a
donation bin
But the kind that are clean
and stay clean a long time after
And after I done that,
I'd fly up in a helicopter
look down at mountain Quilts
I'd go all over the Ozarks
until I find you, wherever you are
Drop down a rope
and bring you home.

I stare down at the page, at my barbed-wire markings all over it.

I was right. This is too big to fix with words. Feel stupid then. Getting my hopes up. Like I can write enough sentences to bandage whatever's gone wrong. Nothing fixed. It is all still jagged like broken glass. And I am still squeezing on its edges, hoping it will not cut me but knowing deep down it will.

13

I walk to Sawyer's first thing. He is up, hitting rocks into the woods with a baseball bat. I can hear him before I can see him, the hollow wooden crack of a bat he got at Booger Holler with his name carved on the side.

"What are you doing?" I say, walking around the edge of the trailer.

"Hittin' stuff."

He has a small pile of rocks in the grass by his feet. He scoops one up, pitches it to himself, then sends it sailing into the woods. I listen to it rattle down the branches of a distant tree.

"Let me hit some," I say.

He hands me the bat. I scoop up a rock. Hit that thing so hard, my elbows hurt. You'd be proud of how hard I hit that rock. It explodes into dust at the end of my bat, sending little pebbles out like a shotgun blast.

Sawyer says, "Hell yeah."

"Sawyer," I say, cutting straight to the reason I walked to his house. "You got to tell me where to find Lukas Fisher."

Sawyer rolls his eyes. "Jesus Christ, Walker."

"They pulled Daddy's truck out of the lake."

"Yeah, but they ain't pulled our *dads* out. They out there somewhere still."

"That's why I got to talk to Lukas."

I can tell Sawyer is getting annoyed. He snatches the bat out of my hand and starts walking away from me. I hurry beside him. Cut him off before he can get back in the trailer.

"Please," I say.

"He's dangerous, Walker."

"I don't care."

By now, I am getting mad too. I can feel it roiling around in me like a pot left on the stove too long. Before I know what I am doing, I grab Sawyer by the front of his shirt and yank him close.

His eyes widen. Then they narrow. "Turn me loose," he says.

"I ain't playing."

He clenches his jaw, and I can tell he is feeling that same roiling anger I am. That's the thing about me and Sawyer. We got the same anger in us. The same anger you have. You put it in me, just like his daddy put it in him. I tighten my grip. He puts one hand around my wrist and starts to twist. We struggle there for a few minutes until he finally breaks free. Then we slam back together like we done back when Coach Widner had us run the Oklahoma Drill. I get his head locked under one of my arms, but he drives his knee into the back of my leg, and we both fall into the mud.

"Stop it!" he says.

Somewhere deep inside me, I want to stop. But I can't. It is like some other person has sat down in the driver's seat of my mind and taken the wheel. I work him to his back and pin his shoulders to the ground. Somewhere along the way I must hit him because Sawyer yelps in pain and small ribbons of blood leak from his nose, from his busted lip. He grunts and hollers and bucks against me, but I have him pinned good.

"Tell me," I say.

That's when he done something I don't expect.

He starts to cry.

Seeing him cry kicks whoever is in control of my brain out of his seat. The real me comes back and takes over. I climb off. Sit on my knees in the mud beside him. The fight is out of him, and he cries hard now, covering his face and turning away from me. I realize he is embarrassed. And I know I'd be embarrassed too for someone to see me carrying on like that. Like a little baby.

"I'm sorry," I say.

He sits up and blinks at me through tears. "I already lost my daddy," he says.

"I know, Sawyer."

"What if you go up there and something bad happens?"

"It won't."

He sits there wiping his eyes with muddy hands, making little sounds like a dying animal. I don't know what to say, so I just sit there, looking at the mud soaking into my jeans. After a minute, he stands and picks up his baseball bat. He stands over me, patting the bat into his hand. If I didn't know him better, I'd hate the way he was holding that bat over me. Sawyer and me might tussle some, but neither is gonna really hurt the other one.

"You're a stupid idiot," he says.

Then he walks inside his trailer and slams the door.

I walk home.

Every time I fight with Sawyer, and I mean the real kind of fighting, not the kind that's just for fun, I feel hollow inside. I can't stand sitting around this house anymore. So I head down the front steps, walk down the dirt road to the highway, and make the long trek into Samson. Takes forever. And it don't help none. All that walking gives my brain an invitation to think. And thinking always circles around you.

When I get to town, I stop at the only gas station and stand around. There's men on a bench out front, smoking cigarettes and drinking coffee. One of them says, "You're Hank's boy."

"I am."

"Was sorry to hear what happened."

"Nothing happened."

"Found his truck, ain't they?" another says, rising slow to his feet, both hands on his knees. "Ole boy was always up to something, I swear to God. Knowed him since he was little."

I don't say anything. There's a pit in my stomach from fighting with Sawyer. And I didn't think it could get any bigger, but hearing them talk about you opens it up so wide I think I might fall in. Disappear. Leave all of me in that hole, let whatever lives down there crawl out instead.

The men are talking to each other more than me now.

"Ain't no wonder his truck wount up in the bottom of that lake."

"Good crappie fishin', Lake Nimrod."

"Shore is. Catch one, you catch thirty."

"Hank got inna that hard licker some bad way."

"Got into a spot worse'n that, I'd say. Damn shame."

"Y'all shut up," I say. But they don't hear me. They rattle on and on about you. Like they know you better than me. There ain't nothing for it, so I stuff it down deep. Turn away from them. Think about going home. But there ain't nothing there for me, so I head farther into Samson, leavin' them dumb idiots on the bench behind me.

I walk past an old building, sagging with age. Stop there and sit down on a concrete step for no reason. There's some businesses behind me. A law firm and the newspaper. A car pulls into a church parking lot across the street, a run-down Ford Mustang. Might have been a nice car once upon a time, but the side panel is primered black while the rest of the car is robin-egg blue, except the hood, which is rusted gray.

The sign in front of the church says *Samson First Freewill Baptist*. We been to that church plenty of times. They have a wooden box out front where you can get donated canned food. The car drives straight to that box. And I feel like I oughta look away. Like I shouldn't watch somebody have this private moment, this moment where they finally admit they need help.

The passenger door opens. Chloe Ennis steps out. She looks around but doesn't seem to recognize me. Then she walks up to the box and starts taking out canned food. It's funny. Not in a ha ha way. It's funny because I was worried she might find out I am poor. But she got to get food from the church donation box too. I guess everybody around here is poor in some way or another.

That night, I sit on the front porch eating an apple I stole from the Dollar General on the way home. I chew all the way down to the core, think about it for a second, then stick the whole thing in my mouth. I lean over the porch railing to spit out seeds. When I look up, Sawyer is standing there.

"Hey, stupid," he says.

Somehow I can tell he's come on good terms. I smile weakly, still feeling guilty, even though you said I ought never show remorse. "Hey, Sawyer."

Sawyer kicks his feet in the grass. "Lukas lives in a trailer off Highway 7. I know 'cause one time Daddy took me out there to drop off some dope."

"Can you take me there?"

"Walker, I'm telling you because we're family. But you ought not go around Lukas, even if he knows something about our daddies."

"I'm trying to help you. And help me."

Sawyer sighs. There is still dry blood on his upper lip. He rubs it with the back of his hand, and it breaks open, leaking fresh blood across his mouth.

"If you're scared, then don't come," I say.

"I ain't scared. But I *ain't* stupid, either."

"So don't come."

Sawyer stands there for a long time. Finally, he says, "I remember we drove down the highway there outside our house, through Dover. I remember going through Dover for sure. We turned on this road, right near this big red barn, where Daddy said they auctioned off cows and horses and stuff like that. Road was called Rushing Road. I remember it because I thought it was a weird name for a road. His trailer was right there. First one you come to. Up on a little hill, with a dirt driveway leading up to it."

I've been to Dover a bunch of times. That is not a short drive. And I don't have wheels. But . . . at least I know where to start looking. I stuff my hands into my War Eagles hoodie, suck my teeth.

"Thanks, Sawyer," I say.

"Don't go up there," he says back.

I shrug. What choice do I have but to go look for you?

Bellwork

In the space below, describe a positive way to deal with negative situations.

_____

The best way I know to deal with bad things is to be keep bad things from happening in the first place. If you are strong enough, nobody can hurt you.

14

Mr. Raines calls me to his office. I figure because they found your truck in the bottom of that lake, and he wants to make sure I am doing alright. But I don't say a single word to him. I cross my arms over my chest and press my lips together tight.

"Are you doing okay, Walker?" he asks.

I don't say anything.

"I'm not upset with you. I just want to make sure you are coping with everything okay."

We listen to the clock ticking.

"Are you writing in your journal? Maybe tried getting it out with a poem or two? Yes? No?" He waves a hand in front of my face. "Not talking to me?"

What does he want me to say? Don't you think it's a little mean to tell a kid he can fix his broken life by writing in a God damn notebook? I wish you'd come up here and tell him off for me. Tell him never to take me out of class and into his office ever again.

During Mrs. Redman's class, I put my head on my desk and watch Chloe Ennis through barely open eyes, but my brain is a hundred miles away thinking about how to get to Rushing Road. During lunch, I go to the library and pull it up on a map. It is almost thirty miles from our farm. That's an impossible walk. I need a ride. Or maybe a bike. Google says it'd take ten hours to walk thirty miles and two or three hours on a bike. That seems doable, but I don't have a bike.

After practice, Coach Widner rolls up in his truck while me and Sawyer are walking home.

God damn Mississippi tags.

Every time I saw Coach Widner during practice, all I could think is him putting his hand on Momma's cheek. So when he rolls down his window and leans out to holler at me and Sawyer, I see the same thing.

"You boys need a ride?" he asks.

"No," I say.

But Sawyer is already halfway to the truck. He opens the door and starts to climb inside. Then he notices I ain't following him. "You coming?"

"I said no."

"Well, there ain't no way I'm walking after running all them gassers."

Coach Widner chuckles, his pooch belly shaking against the steering wheel.

I don't laugh. "Fine."

Sawyer hops in the truck. Coach Widner says, "You sure, Walker? I don't mind."

I'm sure you don't, I think. *Probably heading that way anyway.*

I watch them drive away. Coach Widner's engine roars. Its taillights look like two evil eyes. I tug my backpack strap and begin the long walk home, my eyes down at the tall grass.

It's getting colder. Starting to turn fall, but still hanging on to summer.

You liked this time of year. You *like* this time of year.

When I get to the elementary school, Older Brother and his two sisters are outside. The girls are hanging upside down on the monkey bars, laughing and carrying on without a single care. Makes me wonder if I was like that too a long time ago. I don't remember ever being carefree. And something about that hurts my heart. Like I'm missing out on something every other kid has.

"You alright?" Older Brother says as I walk past.

He don't never talk to us, so I stop in my tracks and look at him. "Yeah, why?"

"You look like you aren't."

"Well, I am, alright?"

"Alright. Fine."

"Bubba, watch me," one of the girls yells. And we both stand there watching as she goes one hand after another across the monkey bars. She drops to the ground, sending little pebbles skittering. "Ta-da!"

Older Brother claps. "That's real good, Mandy."

The younger one scurries up the playset. "Bubba, watch me too!" She grabs the monkey bars and swings out about three rungs, where she gets stuck, kicking her little legs in the air and crying for help.

Older Brother runs over, slips his arm around her waist, and helps her to the ground. "That's real good too, Roo," he tells her. Then he sees I am still watching.

"How come you're always out here with them?" I ask him.

He shrugs. "Makes them happy."

I wish right then I had somebody like him in my life. An older brother. Someone who would do a thing just because it made me happy. I take a deep breath.

Older Brother raises one eyebrow. "You sure you okay?"

"My daddy's missing," I say.

"He the one they pulled his truck out of that lake?"

"Yeah."

He nods slowly. Lets out a long breath. "My momma gone missing too a while back."

"How come?"

"Don't know."

"She coming back, you think?"

He laughs. "Naw. She been gone three years."

We watch the girls play a little longer. There's something good about watching little kids play. Something that warms you up inside. "Well, my daddy is coming back soon."

"Hope so," Older Brother says. "All our pa does is work, even though it don't seem like we get no richer for it. And I know he ain't got no kind of choice in the matter, but somebody has to raise these girls. And you know who raises a kid around here if their parents can't?"

"Who?"

He shakes his head. "Every wind that blows."

I'm not sure I understand. I start to leave. Then I stop and walk back toward him. "Is it hard, raising them up?"

He pulls a box of cigarettes from his back pocket and taps one out. "Feels like getting robbed."

"Then why do it?"

He looks right at me. Tucks the cigarette into the corner of his mouth. "Sometimes you do hard things for people you love."

Name: Walker
Period: 3rd

Bellwork
In the space below, describe something you are passionate
about.

_____

Rodeo

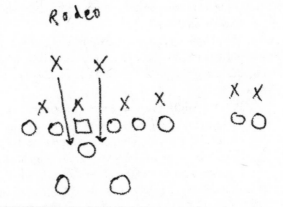

15

This is homecoming week. And that means there's a dance. Never gone to a dance before because I know already every girl in this school would turn me down if I asked. But when I'm looking at one of the handmade posters on the wall, I think about Chloe Ennis.

She don't know me.

She don't know I live on a rotten farm on the edge of the county.

She don't know about you. How you've been in and out of jail for decades. Hell, she probably don't even know you are missing right now.

In other words, she don't know she ought to say no.

The whole time in Mrs. Redman's class, I think about passing her a note. Mrs. Redman is talking about *Romeo and Juliet*, and Chloe is taking notes in the section of her zipper notebook labeled *English*.

I get a crumpled piece of paper from my bag, and I write *Homecoming?* in the center of the page. I fold it up and slide it to the edge of my desk, but I can't think of any way to get her attention.

At the end of class, I palm the note.

I think, *Just talk to her, stupid.*

Everyone starts packing up their backpacks. When the bell rings, I say, "Chloe."

Her green eyes freeze my entire body. I tighten my fist around the note in my hand.

"Yes?" she says.

Everybody filters out of class. Mrs. Redman looks at me, and I think I see a little smile on her face, like she knows this scene. "Are you . . . going to the . . . to the . . ."

Chloe's cheeks turn a little red. Maybe she knows the scene too. "Can I . . . can I?"

God damn it. Why is it so hard to talk sometimes?

"What's your name?" she asks.

"Walker."

"Well . . . walk with me, Walker." She smiles. And I think I'd do anything to make that smile stay on her face forever. I wonder if you felt that way about Momma too. And if you did, how come you stopped?

We leave the classroom.

"Are you liking Samson?" I ask her.

"No. Not really."

"Me either. Why'd you move here?"

"My mom is a lawyer. She's from here, believe it or not. She opened a practice in Little Rock, but she wanted to live where she grew up."

Something about that strikes me funny. I saw her take food from the church donation bin. Don't lawyers make a lot of money? I don't press it though. I'm just happy she is talking to me. Besides, maybe I am wrong. Maybe I don't understand these kinds of things.

"So she just . . . uprooted everything to come home?"

Chloe sighs. "It was her dream."

We pass Sawyer in the hallway. He raises one eyebrow at me, shoots me his missing-tooth smile like he is saying *atta boy*.

"This is my class," she says, stopping. "Did you want to ask me something?"

A world of difference between us. How long can I keep her from finding out who I really am? If we go to homecoming together, will I have to buy her flowers? Will I have to wear a suit? How can I afford any of that?

I scratch the back of my head.

"I just wanted to say welcome to Samson."

She smiles. "You know, you're the first person to say that to me."

Sawyer elbows me at lunch. He says, "You talked to her."

"Yep."

"You ask her to the dance?"

"No."

"Good."

"Why good?"

Sawyer licks his lips. "Because, Walker, I asked Riley Chavers, and she said yes, *and* she's got this cousin in Jasper who said she'd go with you."

I look across the cafeteria. Chloe is sitting by herself at a circle table in the back of the room. She's reading a book called *Carrie*.

"I don't think so," I tell Sawyer.

Chloe reminds me of the punk rock girls I sometimes see on TV. Nothing like the rednecks around here. Maybe that's what I like about her. She is nothing like this place, and every year older I get, the more I hate it here.

Sawyer looks confused. "Why not? Riley can drive. And I was planning on stealing a bottle of whiskey from Momma's cupboard. It'll be a fun time."

"What's her name?"

"Makenzie, I think. They're seniors, Walker. *Seniors.* They gonna drive up and watch us play, then we can go to the dance. And after that . . . *do whatever.* We'll have the whole night with them."

I can tell he isn't going to let it go. Besides, it isn't like I can go with Chloe anyway. I roll my eyes. "Fine, Sawyer. Tell them I'll go. But I ain't wearing a suit or buying flowers."

Coach Widner drives Sawyer home all week. I refuse to get in the truck. Every day this week, he is parked in our driveway with his stupid Mississippi tags. He always says he is there "to help."

But I know the real reason.

On Tuesday, I come in and he's torn up the floor in my room. Now instead of a wet spot, I have a hole that goes straight to the ground.

"What'd you do that for?" I ask.

"What do you think I'm doing?" he says.

I sleep on the couch that night. Figure it'll never get fixed. Like you and the refrigerator. Or how you promised Momma you'd put up new wallpaper after you tore it up with a knife. Next day, I go to school. Talk to Chloe a little in English. Talk to Sawyer. Eat my lunch. Think about the hole in my floor. Think about Lukas. About everything. About you.

After practice Wednesday and after Sawyer and Coach Widner load up and drive away, I hang around the parking lot for a little while. Paton Roper's new BMX is in the bike rack on the front of the building. And I stare at it for a long time. At first, I am thinking, *I wish I had a bike like that. Then I could ride to Lukas Fisher's place.* But the longer I look at it, another thought creeps into my head. *What's stopping me from taking that one?*

I look around.

There is nobody. The line of cars waiting to pick up kids has dwindled to nothing. And I know Paton has extra film study with the assistant coach on account of being the quarterback. When I am sure it is safe, I hurry to the bike, drop down on my knee, and fiddle with the chain. And here's where I get real lucky. I'm not sure how, maybe because Paton Roper is the stupidest kid in the Ozarks, but the lock opens as soon as I tug on it. He must not have latched it all the way by accident. I take it as a sign. I throw the chain in the grass, swing my leg over the seat, and pedal as hard as I can to get home. I blow past the elementary school, past the playground and Older Brother and Mandy and Roo, who are, like always, playing outside.

I know Paton will figure out his bike was stolen right away. And I figure he might suspect me. So I know I have to act fast.

I have to act tomorrow.

Tomorrow, I am going to see Lukas Fisher. Tomorrow I am going to find you.

16

Coach Widner stays until midnight putting down new flooring in my bedroom. I watch over his shoulder, a little amazed.

"You got a bad water leak," he says. "Probably this whole back wall will have to be replaced. Plus the floor in your bathroom is about rotted through completely."

I don't say anything. I watch him work on his hands and knees, replacing all the floorboards he'd pried up with new ones.

"Walker," he says. "Remember this for when you're grown up and out on your own—it is easier to care for something than it is to fix it once it's broken."

I say I understand.

Coach Widner says, "You want to help?"

I shake my head. "I'll just be in your way."

"Next time, Walker. You won't learn if nobody don't teach you."

After he leaves, I get in bed straight away. But I can't sleep. I lie there staring at the ceiling, going over everything in my mind. I have to get up early. Before the sun comes up. I got knots in my stomach over it. Feels like not even one thing can go wrong. And already . . . one thing has. Coach Widner stayed late, and I can't sleep to save my life.

Thirty miles is a long way. Even on a bike. I wake up at five a.m. Stop my alarm clock on the first beep and put my feet on the new floor.

I can hear Momma snoring in the other room, but you never can be too careful. I slip into my sneakers. A hole in the toe. My stomach growls, and even though I expect there to be no food in the cupboards, I open them anyway. There is a box of Pop-Tarts inside, so I stick it in my backpack. I got no clue where the food came from. Maybe Momma stole it. Or got it through some other charity. Maybe Coach Widner.

All I know is I am starved to eat, so I am happy it's there.

Outside, the cold reminds me my War Eagles hoodie is too thin and winter will be here soon. I walk behind the house, where I hid the bike last night. I know you wouldn't ask questions. You'd just laugh and say, "New bike?" And I'd say, "Yup." And that'd be the end of it. But Momma would want to know where it came from. She'd know I'd stolen it. And she'd make me take it back.

I ride to the end of our driveway. Look back at the house one time. The windows still dark. Frost glistening on the roof. Then I turn right on the highway, hammering the pedals around as fast as I can. I ride in silence for a long time, thinking of you, listening to the wind whistle past my head. My cheeks and nose turn cold as snow. A few vehicles pass me, but by the time I reach Dover, maybe an hour later, the sun begins turning the corners of the sky pale blue. More people are out, heading to work or wherever else it is people go so early in the morning. Some old men sit outside the town's only gas station, drinking coffee and smoking pipes on an old bench. One waves at me as I ride past, and I get scared he knows who I am.

Soon, my legs are burning. My heart pounding in my chest. Soon, the sky turns orange and red. Then it turns blue and warm. And more and more cars race down the highway, so close I can feel the wind behind them rip through my hair and clothes. Another half hour maybe, I stop to walk the bike for a while. To tell you the truth, I lose track of time. I am too focused on where I am going, and who is waiting for me when I get there.

Eventually, I pass a huge red barn. A marquee sign out front says *Cattle Auction Saturday*. A little farther on, I come to Rushing Road. This puts new fire in my stomach. New strength in my legs. I hop on the bike, cut through a grass field, and come to the little trailer on a hill, where Sawyer told me Lukas Fisher lives, the last man who ever saw you. The only man I figure can tell me where you went or what happened to you.

There is a dog on the porch. Big pit bull. Sounds like it is saying *rope* over and over as I walk my bike up the driveway. Place reminds me of Sawyer's trailer, but worse. There are cars on blocks in the yard, all busted windows and rusted metal. There's also some farm equipment that looks like it could kill you in a second flat if you got caught inside it.

The whole time I walk up, that dog, saying *rope*.

Rope. Rope. Rope.

My heart starts beating hard in my chest. Little puffs of steam come out of my mouth. I start to think about what Sawyer said. *Lukas Fisher is dangerous. Lukas Fisher come up here waving a gun around.* My mind flashes backward to Momma too. She made me promise to stay away from him. They all know something about him. Something that makes them scared.

I start feeling scared too.

I ain't stupid.

I stop walking. That pit bull yanks on its chain so hard, I think it might pull the entire trailer over. It bounces around, barking and slobbering, its hackles raised up, and I know it isn't just for show. This dog has been raised for meanness.

I remember one time you brought home a puppy. Told me it was our guard dog. Told me it had to be mean because it had to protect the farm. You said a dog becomes whatever you put into it. If you sit around all day talking nice to a dog, petting it behind the ears, and feeding it anytime it's hungry, it grows into a fat lapdog who'll love on everybody who comes around.

"That's fine," you said. "That's *all* fine, if that's all you need it for. But we need this feller for protection. Need him mean. Need him half-starved. Need him damn near ready to bite the head off anybody who don't belong up here."

So you put that dog in our shed. Kicked its ribs when it got under you. Fed it scraps one night each week. And you know what's funny? That dog became what you said it would become. Only, one time it bit you on the leg, and you took it with the shotgun behind the house, and I never saw that dog again.

"Loyalty matters," you said later. "Even with dogs."

Truth is, I was scared of that dog when I was little. And looking at the one on Lukas Fisher's front porch, I imagine he poured every ounce of meanness into that critter you poured into ours. I imagine Lukas opening his front door, slipping the chain from its neck, and turning it loose on me. I am ashamed for you to know how afraid I am.

Lukas appears in the screen door, shirtless. Countless tattoos on his chest and neck. One right across his eyebrows, letters so small I can't read them. Three teardrop tats leaking from the corner of his eye. I see him take me in, his eyes moving up and down. He opens the door and steps outside.

"Be quiet, Ranger," he says, thumping the dog on the head.

But the dog won't stop. Keeps right on saying *rope, rope, rope* at me.

Lukas comes down the steps and stands in the yard. That's when I notice the pistol in his hand. He wets his lips with a blackened tongue. His eyes are hard as marbles. He keeps that gun down at his side, but his finger is on the trigger.

"Who are you and why are you here?" he says, and I can tell from his voice, he has no kindness in him toward me.

"I . . . um . . ." He don't recognize me. A part of me figured he would. But then, I have grown a lot since he last seen me.

"Well? You selling popcorn or something? We don't want none, so go on back where ye came from."

I can't put words together. I don't know why. They get jumbled in my mouth. "I'm here because . . . because . . ."

He throws his hands up, flashing the naked metal of the gun toward me. "Nope. Don't want to hear about your church, don't want to buy wrappin' paper or chocolate or nothin' else you come up here for. Last time I'm going to say it nice."

"Hank Lauderdale," I blurt out. "I'm here about my daddy."

Lukas's emotions change in slow motion. First, he is surprised. Then he looks scared. I swear to you, he looks scared. Somewhere in that grab bag of emotion, I see something else.

A sudden realization. Of who I am. As if I'd just stepped out from behind a curtain.

Then, all that collapses into anger. His hand snaps out, and he grabs my ear and twists until I rise to my tiptoes. He yanks me away from the bike and pulls me close. "Don't you come up here asking about him."

Rope. Rope. Rope.

"Please," I beg, trying to free myself from his grip. I am strong. I *know* I am strong. But he was made strong from a lifetime of hard living. He twists harder, and I fall to my knees. "I need . . . we need . . ."

That dog carries on. *Rope.*

"What you need," he hisses, his voice like snakes slithering, "is to forget about your daddy. Forget you come here. I see you again, it'll be the last time. You hear me? You *understand* me, boy?"

He opens his hand, and I fall in a heap at his feet. He stands over me, the gun still at his side, and I half expect him to kick me like you kicked our old guard dog. Half expect him to shoot me right there. Instead, he walks back to his porch. He hesitates there, bone thin with ropey muscles moving all over his back. He reaches down and takes the chain from the back of the pit bull.

Rope.

"Go on," he says. "'Fore I turn him loose."

17

The whole world is messed up. Makes me want to scream. I sit in class, half expecting Mr. Raines or maybe the principal to call me to his office since I skipped school yesterday. But nobody does. Maybe nobody cares. Maybe I skipped school enough times in my life nobody cares anymore.

Mrs. Redman drones on and on about *Romeo and Juliet.* Keeps on saying they are "star-crossed lovers, on opposite sides of a generational feud."

I listen long enough to hear her say, "Raised from birth to hate. But the great lesson of *Romeo and Juliet* is we don't have to be what our parents raised us to be."

Chloe says, "Yeah, but didn't they die?"

Whole class laughs.

"I'm not trying to be funny," Chloe says. "I mean, if *that's* the lesson of the story, then why'd they have to die?"

"Then what theme do you get from the play?" Mrs. Redman says.

"The opposite. The whole thing is a battle between fate and free will. Romeo and Juliet can't escape their destiny . . . and that's why they have to die."

I can't focus on *Romeo and Juliet.*

Or anything.

I want to stand up and scream at Mrs. Redman.

You think this matters?

This don't matter.

This ain't life or death.

This ain't food in my belly.

I don't say it. Instead, I bite the inside of my cheek. I clench my fists. Open. Close. Open again.

Chloe glances at me. She smiles a little. "What do you think, Walker?" she says.

I can't smile back. Even those green eyes can't shake loose the sour feeling in my stomach.

"Just words in a book," I say. "Don't mean a thing to me."

Chloe frowns.

I put my head on my desk.

Sawyer won't shut up about Lukas Fisher.

"You go see him?" he asked me before school. And again during lunch. "Hey, did you go and see Lukas? What happened?"

I can't bring myself to say *nothing* happened. I can't bring myself to say I ran away like a scared little bird, either.

"He weren't home," I say, while we are getting dressed for tonight's football game.

"Well, best you forget about it, I reckon. Focus on tonight."

I have fire roiling in me. Hot, out-of-control fire. I can see Lukas twisting my ear. Still feel the pain burning down the side of my face. Still see that gun at his side. One other thing I learned about guns yesterday . . . carrying one is always a threat. There is no other way to look at it.

I can't stand the way I crumpled at his feet. How I know if you'd seen that, you'd have felt embarrassed. I make myself focus on the game. Homecoming game. Taking on Harmony Grove.

"Yeah, focus on the game," I say.

Sawyer belly laughs. "No, stupid." He claps a hand on my bare shoulder. "Focus on our *homecoming* dates."

I'd forgotten.

He opens his backpack. There is a bottle of Jack Daniels at the bottom. "It's going to be fun," he says.

"Yeah . . . fun," I say. But I don't mean it.

I can't fix the hole you left in the world when you ran off.

So all I want to do is break it worse.

Coach Widner huddles us up before the game. He says this is the toughest team we've played so far. Right on homecoming.

"You going to let them come in here and take *homecoming* from you?" Coach Widner screams at us.

"No, sir," we say. All on one knee. All in a circle. Him in the middle.

"Listen to me. This is *bigger* than homecoming. Every win is one step closer to where we want to be. And where we want to be is *winning*. This program ain't won a lot, but we can change that. And let me tell you something, winning is contagious. We can't let them take that from us, either. We're gonna go out there, and you know what we're going to do?"

He amps things up. Waving his hands. The other boys eat it like candy. Even Sawyer. I watch him. Eyes getting harder and harder. Leaning forward.

"We're going to punish them," Coach Widner says. "Punish them for thinking they can be on the same field as us. For lining up across from us. For thinking they ever had a chance to win this football game. We are going to play hard. We are going to play fast. And we are going to *punish*."

The boys fly into a frenzy. Someone thuds their helmet on the ground like a drumbeat. Everyone shoots to their feet. We bounce together. Screaming. Roaring like we aren't on our way to play football. Instead, we are on our way to a battlefield. And we are about to kill somebody.

Someone screams, "Punish on three!"

And another counts it down.

One.

Two.

Three.

Kickoff.

Coach has me midrange. Little pooch kick goes to Sawyer, so he takes off in the other direction. I just hit the first person I see. Send them tumbling out of bounds. I can't remember it all. Play out of my mind. Coach Widner slaps my helmet. Sawyer hollers at me. Rain tumbles past the bright stadium lights, running down my helmet and dripping from my facemask. Harmony Grove scores first. Goes up 8–0 on a two-point conversion. They have this running back, a move-in from Conway, we heard is already getting attention from colleges. He blows right past me and Sawyer in our linebacker spots.

Speed kills, they say.

But I am not about to let it happen twice.

Next time Harmony Grove Running Back slips behind the pulling guard, I lower my shoulder into his stomach, lift his legs with both hands, and drive him backward into the mud. Land with a crunch, and we stare at each other. What happens when a boy so fast nobody can touch him meets another so mean nobody gets past him?

Same thing that always happens.

Blood makes the grass grow.

Paton ties the score on an option play, Sawyer running behind him. Paton keeps, because Paton always keeps. He high steps past the cornerback and outside linebacker, who crash on him near the sideline, then tippy-toes fifty yards into the end zone. Sawyer punches in the two-point conversion. Tie ball game at halftime.

I don't want a tie ball game.

I want to crush them.

Punish them, like Coach Widner said.

I think about this during the break. When we go out for the second half, Harmony Grove Running Back scurries to the outside on a buck sweep. His lead blockers try to hem me out, but I crash through them like glass.

Me and Harmony Grove Running Back all alone.

And you already know.

I don't have to say it.

Sheer force of never stopping, never quitting, never-ending anger pours out on Harmony Grove Running Back's body over four quarters of smashmouth football, Coach Widner in my ear hollering *punish, punish, punish.*

You already know.

I *don't* have to say it.

After the game, Coach Widner makes me stand up in front of everybody. Says I held the best running back in the state to less than a hundred yards and one touchdown.

"Aggressiveness," he tells everybody, "is how he done that." Then he laughs. Slaps me hard on the shoulder pads. "And a little meanness. A good linebacker *ought* to be a little mean."

An old beat-up Buick pulls up after the game. Sawyer slugs me on the arm. Grins his missing-tooth smile. He is wearing church clothes, with his long hair slicked back behind his ears. I see the girl behind the steering wheel. Her hair in piles on top of her head. I reckon that must be Sawyer's date, Riley. Another girl hops out of the passenger seat. She wears a denim skirt and boots that go up to her knees, a blouse that shows her shoulders with sparkles on it. She has her brown hair pulled back except for one piece, which hangs down the side of her face like a curled ribbon. She looks at me, heavy blue makeup on her eyelids, and flashes a grin, then gets in the back seat.

I look down at my own outfit. Same thing I wore to school. Pair of jeans. War Eagles hoodie. My hair still wet from my helmet. Sawyer tucks his shirttail, then nods toward the car. "Let's go."

I slide into the back seat. The girl beside me scoots a little closer. "You Makenzie?"

"Walker?"

"Yep."

She nods. "Don't you know homecoming is semiformal?"

"What's semiformal mean?"

She laughs with one hand over her mouth.

Riley drives to the Dollar General down the road and parks in the parking lot. Sawyer unzips his backpack and puts the bottle of whiskey on the dashboard. Light from the parking lot drifts through the windshield, turns orange inside that bottle. Sawyer puts four red plastic cups on the dash and pours a plug of liquor in each. Then he passes them out.

Riley downs hers in one gulp. "Cheers," she says.

Makenzie laughs, pours hers down her throat too. Sawyer

glances at me, smiles, and tips his cup back. I shrug and pour the bitter liquid into my mouth. Think of you. Think of Lukas Fisher. His yard. My ear. That dog. A wooden taste fills my mouth, burns all the way down. Sends me drifting backward through time, back to when you were home almost every night but still drinking. I would find you out on the porch sometimes, sitting with your feet hanging off, bottle half-drank beside you. You'd give me sips sometimes and laugh when I gagged. I hated the taste but liked seeing you laugh, so I kept drinking. Momma sure did yell when I fell in the kitchen and she realized I was drunk. Maybe seven years old, I think.

Makenzie takes a pack of smokes from her purse and taps one out. We share the cigarette in the back seat.

"You okay?" Makenzie says, soft in her voice. And I wonder if this is a power all women have. To put such tenderness in their voice you want to pour everything out at their feet.

I take a drag on the cigarette. "No."

"You want to talk about it?"

I exhale smoke and hand the cigarette to her. "No."

She puts her head on my shoulder, and my heart thumps hard in my chest. I smell perfume and smoke. "You played great tonight, Walker. Sawyer said you was something to see on the football field. Said you was meaner than anyone out there. I thought he was just building you up, but no. It's true. I was impressed."

Riley turns in the seat. "Y'all ready to go?"

"Guess so," I say.

Riley puts the car in gear and drives back toward the school. On the way, Sawyer takes a long pull straight from the whiskey bottle, then passes it to me. I look at the liquid for a long time. Feel it already burning inside me. Blurring the edges of the world.

I put the bottle to my lips and drink.

Riley drives around the high school and parks in front of the gymnasium. My head spins. She parks, and I step out, stagger, and catch myself.

"Do we have to go to this dance?" I ask.

"You want to skip to the end?" Sawyer says. I don't see it, but I know he is giving me that crooked, missing-tooth smile of his.

The girls laugh.

Makenzie grabs my arm. She squeezes my bicep. "Come on, Walker. I want to dance."

Inside, music blares. Everybody moves in strobe lights. I see teammates. Kids I know from class. They bump shoulders. Grind their bodies together. Riley pulls Sawyer into the crowd, and I do not see them again. The world blurs around me. Makenzie pulls me to the dance floor, laces her arms around my neck. I put my hand on the small of her back, surprised how little she is between my arms. She presses against me. Whispers, "Loosen up a little."

The room spins around me. Her lips graze my ear. Send shivers down my body. I start to move. The music makes my insides shake. I keep thinking, *She ain't Chloe, but she's here. She's here, and she likes me, and she's pretty, and she's alright.*

What it feels like is this: I never want Chloe Ennis to know the real me, because I know if she did, she wouldn't like me. But Makenzie? She is the same as me. Poor, white trash. And she knows who I am because I am like her too. I don't have to pretend to be anything else.

And that's . . . alright, I reckon.

Easier, if nothing else.

We dance. And I laugh in a way I haven't since before you disappeared. The laughing comes easier, but the whole thing is surrounded in fuzz, a blur, like I am inside a fuzzy blanket on a cold day.

Blur.

Dance.

Blur.

Her lips on mine.

Blur.

"Well, hey, Walker," a familiar voice.

Sudden clarity.

Chloe Ennis. Her hair pulled up. And I think she has makeup on. Her green eyes flash at me, and I see a little extra kindness there. Like maybe . . . just maybe . . . she is glad to see me.

Or maybe I am just drunk.

I smile back, for *sure* happy to see her. Makenzie puts her fists on her hips and rolls her eyes.

Paton steps behind Chloe. Puts his hand on her back.

"This is my date," Chloe says.

"You're together?" I ask.

"Yes."

Yes . . .

That word sends me tumbling back into the blur. I can't remember much else from that night. The rusty Buick. That bottle of whiskey. *She's Alright Makenzie* tugging on my arm. Headlights painting trees passing too fast. Riley driving. Bendy roads through the Ozarks. "This is dangerous," someone says. Maybe me. And everyone laughs. An overlook. Makenzie kissing me, her lips warm and soft. Pressing into me. Her hands on my chest. Our tongues touching.

Blur.

Blur.

Nothing.

someone said I ought to be mean
like that dog daddy locked in our shed
turned that hound into something cruel
something from my bAd dreAms

wonder what shed you put me in
to make me like thAt dog.

what goodness I missed but other
boys got?

what makes a heart good?
and what makes one bad?

everything, I figure

everything.

18

Can't find Sawyer Saturday morning. Walk all over the woods. Then I stop and listen. Hear the *pop, pop, pop* of a distant pistol. Follow that sound. And sure enough, Sawyer is standing in a clearing, shooting that old gun his daddy snatched from Lukas a while back.

Sawyer is shooting at nothing at all. Just reeling off bullets. *Pop. Pop.* Stopping. Reloading. Reeling off some more. He doesn't hear me walk up. Not even when I say his name two times.

I have to touch his shoulder.

"Good Lord, Walker," he says. "You scared the hell out of me."

I grin. "What are you doin'?"

"Shooting."

"At what?"

Sawyer shrugs. "Nothing, I guess. Just letting off some steam." He itches the back of his head with the tip of the gun.

"Don't point that gun at your head," I tell him. "God damn, Sawyer."

His cheeks turn red. I know he knows better.

"You feeling better?" he asks me. "I was hungover bad."

"I feel like I always feel."

"You have fun?"

I shrug. Some parts of the night were fun. Other parts cling to me like burs. Digging into my skin. Only, I can't pluck them out and throw them away. They're here to stay. When I sobered up, I kept going back to how I felt around Makenzie.

Like myself.

And around Chloe?

Someone else. Someone *better*.

I wonder which is right. To be with someone who accepts you exactly as you are? Or to be with someone who makes you want to be better? I think about it hard, but I never can decide which.

"Can I shoot?" I ask Sawyer.

He hands me the gun. I look into the distant trees. I fire six times at nothing.

When we get to his trailer, there is a truck parked in the driveway. Aunt Maybelle is outside with a man we don't know. She works her hands together like a cartoon cat hungry for a meal. When we get close, she says, "You two get in the truck."

"Where we going?" I ask, hoping she might say to get some food. If Coach Widner doesn't stock our pantry, weekends are endless hours of my stomach eating itself up, my entire body begging me to put something in my mouth and chew. Momma doesn't always tell him when we are out of food. I think she's embarrassed.

Sawyer's momma says, "You remember Jody Caughron? Used to go to church when you were little?"

I don't. Neither does Sawyer.

"Well, he's dead. Got permission to go clean some things out of his house."

The man we don't know nods and gets in the truck. Sawyer glances at me. Raises one eyebrow the way he does when he isn't sure about something. But what can we do? She says we have to go help. So we do.

We ride in the truck for maybe an hour, down county roads, crossing a creek so wide and so rapid, I worry in secret we might get swept away. We get to this old white house, deep in the country, paint peeling off the front porch. The door hangs on one hinge and moss grows up one side of the roof. An old orange cat sits on the porch, swishing its tail around and blinking slow.

The man I don't know says, "Welp," and turns the truck around in the yard. He backs all the way up to the front steps, hops out, and lowers the gate.

Aunt Maybelle turns to us. "Take as much as you can and load it up in the truck back there."

"Why are we out here?" Sawyer asks.

"Family said we could," she says quickly. I notice her eyes look away from us.

Sawyer seems to believe her. But I am reminded of the time we stripped copper from that house in the woods, when you said you had permission, but I don't really think you did.

My stomach growls hard as I walk to the front door.

The orange cat hides under the porch as I take the steps.

Inside, I look around. Little porcelain baby dolls on shelves all over the walls. Old VHS movies. Magazines and books everywhere. Whole place smells like cat piss. There's a wheelchair in the corner. An oxygen tank with yellowed tubing coiled all over the place.

"Jesus Christ," I say. There's not a lot of houses worse than ours. But this is one of them.

I walk to the kitchen, slipping past Aunt Maybelle in the doorway.

"There ain't nothing here," the man I don't know says.

"Gotta be something," Aunt Maybelle says.

I walk to the refrigerator. Open it. A whole case of soda. I crack a can open and chug it down fast. Then I find a package of hot dogs, the package split open between the links with a knife. Only two of the hot dogs hardened with age. I stuff six of them into my mouth one right after the other, chewing so loud Aunt Maybelle gives me a dirty look. "Manners," she says.

Manners.

Can you believe that?

I fill two plastic grocery sacks with leftover food. A bag of chips. Some bologna. A whole package of ramen noodles. Six boxes of mac and cheese. A frozen pot roast from the freezer. Carry everything out to the truck and put it where I'd been sitting.

I go back inside, navigate through towers of books and magazines and broken porcelain dolls, to a bedroom in the back of the house. Stuff in piles everywhere. Those big rubber bins you buy at Walmart, just stuffed with things. Christmas decorations. Old clothes. Old sewing patterns like Memaw used to buy. I shimmy through and move boxes to reach the back of the room. There is a chest of drawers in the corner. I go through each drawer one at a time. Old family photographs mostly. When I open the bottom drawer, my mouth falls open. A black lockbox. A little silver key right on top. I get on my knees and pick up the key, my fingers shaking.

A lockbox is where you put important stuff. Things you don't want nobody else to find.

I stick the key in the lock and turn it. Lift the lid. Inside, there are stacks of money. I pick them up. Twenty-dollar bills. Five-dollar bills. A fifty. A one-hundred-dollar bill. I start counting.

One hundred . . .

Two hundred . . .

Three hundred . . .

The man I do not know comes into the room. He can't see the money on account of all the stuff piled around.

"What's back there?" he asks.

I hold the money tight in my fist. "Some toys," I say. "Action figures. Superheroes and stuff."

He chuckles. "Yours now if you want."

I stuff the wad of money in my coat pocket. He stands between piles of junk, shifting his weight from one foot to the other.

"Nah," I say. "That's baby stuff."

The whole way home, I think about the money in my pocket.

"Things are about to change for us," Aunt Maybelle says, her feet up on the dash. Happy in a way I ain't seen her in ages.

"They are?" Sawyer says. "How come?"

"Once things shake out, Sawyer, you and me are about to come into some big money."

"Shake out?"

She turns up the radio. "Let Momma worry about it. Just know the winds of change are blowing. And for the first time in maybe my whole damn life, I am going to be on top."

Sawyer sits on the seat beside me. He shrugs, like *what the hell is she talking about?* I shrug back. I don't know, and I don't care.

Sawyer has a PlayStation in a brown paper bag on his lap, plus five or six sports games and one where you steal cars and shoot people and fight the police. He's excited. I am too. Because I know I ain't going to bed hungry. And I know I'll get to play those games with him too. And I know you'd be mad to hear this next part, but already I know I ain't giving that money to Momma. I know she needs it real bad. But if I give to her, she'll wonder where it came from. She might say something to her sister. And then they'd know I kept the money for myself.

I have a better plan for it.

A plan that might fix things. A plan to bring you back to us.

After that, you can tell your brother, Wyatt, we ain't leaving the farm. Tell him to stick it where the sun don't shine. You can go back to work and get us a new truck. You can come to all my football games and see how mean and tough I am. You can tell Coach Widner to stay on the sideline and away from Momma. You can fix our refrigerator. Daddy, when you get back, I'll *help* you fix the refrigerator. I swear to *God* I will. When you get back, you won't ever have a lick of attitude from me ever again. I'll do like you say the first time you say it, I swear. If you come back. I swear.

19

They call me to the principal's office on Monday. Mr. Raines is there. Feel sick as soon as I see him. They leave me alone outside the office for a long time. I listen to the clock tick, tick, tick. Think about the money wadded up in a fat envelope in the pocket of my War Eagles hoodie. One thousand dollars total. The most money I've had at one time in my life. I wonder if they know. If somehow they know I have this one good thing, and they want to take it away from me.

Principal opens the door. His eyes are vacant. Like a cow or some other stupid animal. He says, "Come on in here, son." Principal's a big old boy. Shirt barely fit around his belly. He sits down and crosses one leg over the other. Grunting and panting. Then he chews the end of a pen and stares at me.

Mr. Raines sits in a chair nearby, his arms folded across his chest. His right leg bounces and shakes. Just like Memaw's used to do. He sees me looking, makes a face, and hitches his left leg over his right. It's still not enough. The tremble keeps going. He taps one finger on his forearm over and over, a frown on the corner of his mouth.

"You know anything about a missing bike?" Big Belly Principal says after a while. "Belonged to Paton Roper. Disappeared after football last week. You know anything about that?"

I remember one time we picked you up from the jail. You hopped in the car, acting like it wasn't a big deal. Momma was real mad at you. Asking where you been. That time, you went missing for two weeks before you finally turned up.

That's why I don't believe for one second you are dead.

It's why I know you'll either turn up and spend the next couple weeks winning Momma over with nice words and flowers and hugs, or we'll have to find a way to bail you out of jail again. And if that's the case, it'll take you twice as long to get back in Momma's good graces, believe me.

I remember when we picked you up last time, you said to me, "Walker, if a cop says you done something wrong, don't admit it, even if they say they got proof. That's *good* legal advice, boy. Don't even *talk* to them."

Back then, I didn't know what you meant.

But I find out real quick.

Big Belly Principal uncrosses his legs and leans across the table. Laces his fingers together and tries to look tough. Tries to look the way you look tough. But I've weathered your hard looks all my life, and he got nothing on you.

"Walker," he says. "We got you on camera taking that bike."

"No, you don't," I say. "Because I didn't take it."

"Paton thinks you did."

"Am I on camera, or did Paton tell you he *thinks* I took it?"

Big Belly Principal and Mr. Raines look at each other.

I feel nervous then. Like maybe Big Belly Principal is going to turn around his computer screen and show a security video of me stealing that bike. I can't tell them about the bike. Even if I want to. I *need* the bike more than Paton anyway. His daddy'll just buy him a new one. Probably a better one. So why's it matter if I have it hidden behind the shed at our farm? I need that bike so I can go back to Lukas Fisher's trailer. Take him that money I found and tell him he can have it . . . but only if he tells me where I can find you.

Mr. Raines looks sad. And that bothers me some. I'm not sure why. Big Belly Principal lets out a breath. Half grunt, really. Says, "It's going to be better for you if you tell the truth."

"I done told it."

"Mr. Jordan," Mr. Raines says, leaning closer to Big Belly Principal. "Mr. Lauderdale here has been showing a lot of progress in counseling. He's keeping a journal to get out his negative feelings.

And I've spoken to his teachers, and they all say he's shown a marked improvement in all of his classes."

I clench my jaw to keep my mouth from falling open.

I can't believe he stood up for me. I like him more right then. But also, I feel sick in my stomach. Because even though he's defending me, I really do have the bike.

I watch Big Belly Principal's gears spin for a minute. Finally, he says, "Fine. But, Walker, if you decide you have something you want to tell us . . . my door is right here."

I get up to leave. I look at Mr. Raines. He looks back at me. I walk straight to his office, just a little bit down the hallway. I stick my hand in my pocket and feel the wad of bills. I check both ways to make sure I am alone. I remember the medical bill on his desk, how I asked him about it to make him uncomfortable, and he frowned and said he'd have to get creative to pay it. I think about him shaking during the meeting. I think about Memaw. Maybe it's too late, but I want to help. I want to say *thank you* for standing up for me. I take a hundred-dollar bill and slide it under Mr. Raines's door.

At practice, I play scout team linebacker, even though I'm the starter. I like it because Paton Roper plays quarterback. And in our Dead-T offense, the quarterback runs the ball sometimes.

Coach Widner says my "motor runs on one speed." He says I ought not hit the quarterback. Even gives Paton a little red jersey to wear over his shoulder pads, so we can tell it's him in the scramble of things at the line of scrimmage and remember *not* to hit him.

Paton slides under center. Hollers *hut* to start the play. The left guard and left tackle pull to my side. Behind them, the halfback sweeps the same direction. The whole thing like a door opening, pushing defenders out of the way. Paton Roper is behind that door. Letting the big men do the work for him. And even though I'm not supposed to hit him, I crash through his lead blockers like a wrecking ball, knocking the left guard on his rear. Paton yelps like a hurt animal when I hit him.

I shove his helmet into the ground when I stand up.

Coach Widner pushes through kids, blowing his whistle over

and over. He yells in my face, "Don't hit the damn quarterback, Walker!"

I glare at him. Think about him driving his truck to our farm. Getting cozy with my momma.

"Boy, what is wrong with you?" he says.

I don't answer.

He puts his hands on his hips. "Bear crawl," he says. "One hundred yards. Go."

Takes me the rest of practice to crawl a hundred yards without letting my knees touch the ground. I know if Coach Widner catches me resting, or sees me baby crawling, he'll make me start over. One hundred yards doesn't seem like much when you look at it. But when you're bear crawling, it's an eternity.

After practice, I don't wait for Sawyer.

I don't wait for him because I know Coach Widner will be out soon. And he will want to know if I need a ride home. And Sawyer will go with him like always. And I'll take the slow walk home and get angry about it.

It's cold out. Can see my breath. Little thin ice sheets over all the puddles. Crunch some up good as I walk past. When I get to the elementary school, I can see the kids outside. The littlest one, Roo, has on an oversized coat. Older Brother has on a tank top undershirt. He stands nearby shivering.

"What are you doing?" I ask, as I get closer. "Ain't you cold?"

"Very."

"Why you out here, then?"

He nods toward his little sisters swinging on the swing set. Laughing. "They always want to come over here."

"Tell them it's too cold."

He laughs. "It makes 'em happy. Roo outgrew her coat, so I gave her mine. It's too big, but that's better than too small."

I stand there for a long time. Something about watching those little girls play, about their brother standing by shivering, never failing to smile at them when they call his name. It makes me think of you.

Actually . . .

It makes me think about how you were *nothing* like that.

"Listen," I say. Feeling around in my coat pocket.

Older Brother raises an eyebrow.

I hand him two one-hundred-dollar bills. "Take this and get them some warm clothes. It's gonna get even colder soon."

He hesitates. "What do you want for this?"

"Nothing."

"Where'd it come from?"

I try to be calm. I look away from him. "It's mine."

Older Brother takes the money. He tucks it into his pocket. Then, standing there, his bottom lip quivers one time. I look into his eyes. Red-rimmed. A single tear breaks free and drips across his cheek. He wipes it away fast. Then turns away from me.

"I got to go," I say, feeling uncomfortable.

When I get some distance away, he calls out, "Hey, you."

I turn, and he jogs up to me. Puts a hand on my shoulder.

"Thanks," he says. "You have no idea what this means to us."

20

Take off on the bike before the sun comes up. Even colder today. Wind coming down off the mountains. Howling and spitting little raindrops, so cold they sting my face as I pedal. The gas station in Dover is open, so I stop in and buy a cup of coffee and a donut with some of the money in my pocket. I stick the change in my pants pocket instead of my coat pocket. I want to keep it separate, maybe not even tell Lukas I have it. That way, I can use the money to buy food later.

I walk outside. One of the old men on the bench says, "Nice bike," and I get worried he knows I stole it. I look down at the coffee. See my face looking back at me in a black circle. I've never tried coffee before. But you drank it. Black. Without sugar. Because you said that's how men drink their coffee.

I take a sip. Burn my tongue. Nearly gag.

The men on the bench laugh at me.

Why is it everything you said I ought to do because it's "what men do" hurts in some way or another?

I slurp down the rest of the coffee. Toss the Styrofoam cup in the trash and hop on my bike. I can feel those old men's eyes on me as I ride away. Do they know where I am going? Do they know who I am? Where I got this bike? Those are things I think about until that gas station dips under the rolling hills behind me, and I can't see it no more.

Lukas's old pit bull goes plum crazy the moment I come around the corner.

Rope. Rope. Rope.

I stop at the edge of the yard and get off my bike. This time, a woman comes to the door. She's wearing a Led Zeppelin T-shirt and a pair of shorts, and even though it's cold as hell out here, she steps outside. The dog stops barking, stares up at her like it's asking permission.

"You lost, honey?" the woman says, and her voice sounds like a million cigarettes.

"No, ma'am. I come up here to talk to Lukas about something."

She frowns, her skin wrinkling like a brown lunch sack. "Well, who are you, then?"

"Hank Lauderdale was my daddy."

Her eyes widen a little bit. She licks her lips. "You better run off."

"Ma'am," I say, pleading with her. "Please. I just want to talk to him."

"I don't think so."

"Tell him . . . tell him I've got money."

Her face softens a little. "How much?"

"Six hundred." I try to beg her with my eyes.

She goes back inside without a word. A few minutes later, Lukas steps out on the porch. He looks at me with little black eyes. Like a shark. Like he wants to tear me to shreds for being here again. This time, he don't have a gun.

"What are *you* doing here?" he says.

"Lukas, sir, I just want to know where my daddy is."

"I told you—"

"I know you did, but . . ." My heart hammers. The woman steps outside behind him. She leans against the side of the house and reaches down with one hand to scratch that pit bull between the ears. That horrible dog turns into a puppy. Like magic. Its tongue comes drooping out of its mouth. Its eyes bunch up. Almost looks like a smile.

"But what?" Lukas barks.

"I have money. You can have it. Just tell me what you know."

The woman walks a few steps closer to Lukas. She drapes an arm around his shoulder. Whispers something in his ear. He nods slowly. Then he walks down the steps toward me.

Everything inside me screams to run.

But I stand firm.

I stay tough.

You would be proud.

When he gets close to me, he holds out his hand. "Give it here."

I wait a few seconds. I'm not sure I'm doing the right thing. I think of Momma. This money could feed us for a month. Maybe two, if we stretched.

"Give it here," Lukas says again, his voice harder.

I hold the wad of money in my fist. It's like my fingers don't want to let go. Deep down, I know this is stupid. Know I can't trust Lukas. But what choice do I have? And what good will a few hundred dollars do me in the long run, anyway, if I can't find you?

Lukas snatches the bills from my hand. I stand there and watch him count it. Watch his face get greedy. Already imagining what he will spend it on. When he's finished, he shoves the money in his pocket.

"What's a boy like you doing with this kind of money?" he asks.

"I saved it up."

Lukas laughs. "You really are stupid."

"Stupid?"

"I don't know shit."

A cold wind blows. Rustling his long hair. He stares at me with those black eyes, a little smile messing up his features. Rain comes a little harder now. Soaking through my jacket. Lukas walks back to the trailer and steps under the porch, out of the rain. He hands the money to the woman. The dog whines and thumps its tail.

I hurry closer. The dog shoots to its feet and bristles.

"Last text Daddy sent my momma was a photo. You was in it," I say.

The dog says *rope* one time, but the woman puts her hand on its head, and it stops.

Lukas turns toward me. "Sure, I seen your daddy. Drove to Blackwater. Had some drinks. Other things. But that don't mean I know where he's gone now."

"You *have* to know something."

"No, I don't."

"Please . . ."

Lukas folds his arms across his chest. "Leave."

"No, please . . . you have to *know* something."

"I said leave." He starts to go inside. I swallow my fear and run up the front steps. I grab him by the wrist. He spins to face me, like he thinks I want to throw fists. A wicked smile crosses his face.

"I . . . paid you," I say.

The dog barks again so close, I can feel the heat from its mouth, the spit on my face.

Lukas screams in my face, "I can't tell you what I don't *fucking* know."

I think for a second he might hit me, but the woman pushes past him. She puts her hand on my shoulder. Soft. Not hard. She guides me away from the dog and away from Lukas.

"I know you're hurting," she says.

I don't say nothing.

"I'd be hurting too," she says. "Look, I don't know if Lukas knows a damn thing about your daddy. Could be he does. But could be he's telling you the truth right now."

"He's gotta know," I say. "He was with him. Even just telling me where to look next or who to ask. *Anything.*"

"Listen, honey." Her voice is like sugar. And I can tell, maybe a long time ago, minus all the cigarettes and drugs, she had been beautiful. And maybe there was still beauty in there somewhere, hidden inside. I think so. Somewhere in her eyes. "My name is Sherry Whitmire. And you're Walker Lauderdale? Now we know each other."

I nod.

She glances over her shoulder at Lukas, still watching us from the porch, the dog growling and carrying on. Rain trickles down from my head, between my eyes, and off the tip of my nose. I think maybe I can cry now. Break open some hard spot inside me and let it pour out. Maybe she'll see how hurt I am. How hurt you made me when you left. And she'll want to help.

"I'll work on him, okay?" she says. I don't know what she means.

She can tell I am confused, so she adds quickly, "I'll find out what he knows. And I'll get it to you somehow."

I nod.

"I had a boy like you," she says.

"Had?"

"He's grown." Her eyes fill with tears. And I think maybe he's grown into something she don't like or recognize. He left the sweet baby boy she'd rocked to sleep behind and become the same as all the other men around here.

The same as I'm becoming, I guess.

She smiles easy. "You're a good kid, Walker," she says. "Don't lose that."

21

keep wondering what I will do when I find you. What will I ask you? I'm all mixed up inside over it. I'm mad at you. But I'm . . . *sad* at you too. I thought we was family. You always said nothing matters more than family. Then you run off.

Sink our truck.

Here one day.

Gone the next.

I can't get my brain around it.

Keep thinking you'll be on the couch one morning, a little collection of beer cans on the floor around you. Like so many mornings before. Then I wake up and hurry to the living room.

But you ain't there.

You're never there.

After football practice, I skip the ride home from Coach Widner again. This time, Older Brother and his sisters aren't outside. I was hoping they would be. Hoping I'd see them in new pairs of shoes. New sweaters. I was hoping they would be smiling, and that smile would get down inside of me and break open the awful feeling in my stomach.

I remember I have extra money in my pocket from yesterday, the change from that coffee I bought and stuck in my pocket instead of my hoodie. I walk to the Dollar General and buy junk food—a few bags of gummy worms, some nacho-flavored tortilla chips, and a couple two liters. I still have fifty bucks in my pocket when I am done. I decide right then, I'll give that money to Momma.

But when I get home, Coach Widner's truck is in my driveway. Mississippi tags. The door to the house is locked and the curtain pulled tight over the window. I listen through the glass but don't hear anything. I bang on the door, but no one answers.

I put down the bags of food. Pick up a rock from the driveway. Without thinking about it, I wing it through the living room window. It punches a clean hole through the glass.

Momma throws open the front door and yells at me. "What is *wrong* with you?"

Coach Widner appears behind her. I pick up another rock and throw it at him. He ducks, and it disappears through the open door behind him. I hear something break inside. Momma hurries down the steps.

"Stay away," I warn.

"Your coach is trying to *help* us, Walker."

"He can help by staying out of our house with the door locked."

Momma got anger in her too. You know that. You seen it plenty. You and her used to go back and forth so loud. Having your secret talks outside that weren't so secret because I could hear them through my bedroom window. Her yelling and screaming. You yelling and screaming right back. I can see that anger in her now. Her cheeks turn bright red like she's been slapped. She sticks her finger right in my face.

"No respect," she says. "You got no respect. I'll tell you that right now."

Her voice doesn't sound like Momma at all. Sounds like someone who hates me.

Coach Widner walks down the front steps. "Hey, now," he says. "Hang on."

But Momma doesn't hang on. She looks straight at me. Doesn't blink. And I know she picks these next words carefully. Picks these words out of the millions of words that exist. She picks them because these words are the perfect shape and sound to wiggle down inside me and destroy everything.

"You want to know what your problem is?" she says. "You want to know? I'll tell you. You got *too much* of your father in you."

I know you'd have hollered right back. But I don't have the words. I scoop up the bags of junk food I bought and run down our driveway. All the way to the highway. Then I run some more. When I get to the turnoff toward Sawyer's, I go up that way.

When I knock on his door, he answers. I hold out the food. "Can I stay here tonight?"

"You don't gotta ask."

That feels good right there. To know that no matter what else, I have Sawyer on my side. Like a brother but better. Closer. I step inside his little home. And even though it's smaller than our farm, dirtier and stuffed to the brim with even more junk, I feel better than I've felt all day. I feel safe. Like I've gone somewhere that might could protect me for a change.

I sit down on the couch.

"Where's your momma?" I ask.

Sawyer scoops up the bags of junk food. He pulls out a package of sour gummy worms. "Score," he says.

"Where's your momma?"

"Don't know. You want to play PlayStation?"

I feel small again that night. But not in a bad way. I mean small like a little boy. The way the world is curious about you and you're curious about the world. And all the scary things out there seem far away. Like they can't touch you.

We play that PlayStation until three in the morning. Football games. Sawyer beats me three times. He plays as the Kansas City Chiefs. I play as the Dallas Cowboys because that's your team. Then we play a game where you steal cars and run over people and do whatever cutting up you can until Sawyer drops the controller and says, "I can't keep my eyes open."

We sleep right there on the floor. Junk food all around us.

I dream about you. Only in the dream, you ain't gone. You're big, and I am small. And you put me on your lap. And I think how nice it would be to stay there. Your big arms around me. Nobody's gonna mess with you. And if they ain't going to mess with you, then they ain't going to mess with me, either.

I wake myself up smiling. Sit up in the dark. Blink until I can see. But there ain't nothing to see.

Not really.

me and my best friend
    brother
like a secret holder
who knows without saying
for as much as we pretend different
it don't feel good To Be Strong

feels like ice on your bones.

22

oach Widner throws a pair of work gloves on the bed next to me. I've been lying there, staring at a water spot in the ceiling, thinking about things.

I raise an eyebrow at him. "What's this?"

"Come on," he says. He waits in the doorway for a minute, then puts on his coach voice. "I *said* come on."

I grab the gloves and stand up. Follow him into the living room. We go outside, and I see a new window leaning against the house, near the one I punched a hole in yesterday.

"What's going on?" I ask.

"Your momma has a hard enough time keeping food in your belly without you breaking things and costing her even more money," Coach Widner says.

I start to protest, but Coach Widner shakes his head. "No, Walker. There's no excuse. You were mad. So what? Being mad ain't an excuse to do whatever fool thing comes into your head."

"I know what you were doing in there," I say.

He scowls, motions toward the window. "You're going to help me fix this. And you're going to have a good attitude about it. You understand?"

What does he think he's doing? Trying to be you? Trying to teach me a lesson? Well, I've had enough lessons to last me my entire life. I glare at him. Clench my jaw.

"Understood?" he says again. And when I still don't say anything, he says, "You want to play in tomorrow's game, or would you rather ride the bench?"

My hands start shaking. I feel the heat inside me the same way I did when I threw that rock through the window. But what can I do? I *have* to play tomorrow. I fight hard to throw water on that fire . . . at least long enough to get through fixing this stupid window.

Coach Widner picks up a roll of blue painter's tape. He hands it to me.

"Take two strips and make an X across the glass," he says, tugging on his own pair of work gloves. "When we push that window out, it's going to want to shatter because of the hole you put in it. The tape keeps it together."

I take the tape and make an X. "Now what?"

"Go inside and do the same thing again."

I sigh, annoyed. "How long is this gonna take?"

"Longer if you piss and moan the whole time."

I walk inside. Momma's on the couch with a cup of coffee in both hands, watching everything through the window. She looks amused. I point at her. "Why you let him do this to me?"

"Do what?"

I wave a hand toward the broken window.

"Walker, you might learn something."

Coach Widner pecks on the glass. He taps his wrist. I glance at Momma one more time, then rip off two pieces of tape to make an X on the backside of the glass. When I get back outside, Coach Widner says, "There you go. I'll do this next part."

I sit down on the porch. Coach Widner rummages around in a toolbox until he finds a box cutter knife. He leans against the house and sticks the blade into a crease around the window and starts sliding it around. "These windows are sealed up with silicon, Walker. So you gotta cut it loose."

I can't tell you how much I don't care. "What are you trying to do with my momma?"

Coach Widner finishes what he is doing before he speaks again.

"Walker," he says, snapping the box cutter closed with a thumb. "I care about your momma. That's all. I don't know where any of this is heading, but I do know I care about her."

Coach Widner brushes past me on his way inside. I stay on the porch, chewing on his words. Momma deserves someone to care about her, but I can't help the sour feeling in my stomach and chest. Inside, I can see Coach Widner sliding that razor blade around the window. After a few minutes, he gives it a push, and just like he said, the whole thing shatters. Only . . . that tape he had me stick across the glass keeps it together. The whole mess hits the ground with a rattle.

I look at Coach Widner through the hole in the wall. He smiles, his teeth flashing in the dark.

"Some stuff seems harder to fix than it is," he says.

23

We take the long road to Yell County, up toward Petit Jean, where you used to take us when you felt like hiking the waterfall trail there. I think about you the whole drive, how you'd breeze through these winding roads, the radio blaring Garth Brooks. You'd sing along at the top of your lungs. When I was little, I'd sing with you. When I got older, I felt embarrassed. But riding up these roads, my head in my hands, I think I'd give anything to hear you sing like that again. We have a game against the Hanover Little Johns. And this is one I know you'd have circled on the calendar . . . if you were still here.

Before the game, Coach Widner huddles up in the locker room.

"You know how many times we've played Hanover over the years?" he said. "I looked it up. I went back and checked. We have played the Little Johns every year since 1935. That is more than eighty or ninety games. Think about that. Your daddies. Your daddies' daddies. On that field out there. Against those same guys. If that ain't a rivalry, then I don't know what is."

I think about it all during warm-ups. I know you played here. You told me all about it. Played corner, you said. And wide receiver. Y'all was pretty good, you said. Made it all the way to the semifinals of the state tournament your senior year of high school. That's the furthest any team from Samson has ever gone.

I look up at the visitor bleachers. One thing I'll say about Samson—small as it is, we travel well. There's enough folks in the stands from our school it could have been a home game. Hanover's just down the road a little ways. And what else is folks gonna do on a Friday night besides watch their boys war against the boys down the road?

I watch the Hanover Little Johns run plays on the other side of the field. Coach Widner said all week during practice their spread offense was designed to trick me, but I can't remember how. I stopped listening to him when he started showing up at our house every day, locking the door.

You always hated this kind of tricky football. Always said it wasn't *real* football. You liked smashmouth football. Football where it came down to who was meanest. Who won the battle in the trenches. Who hit harder. You liked football where the offense said to the defense, *We're gonna run the ball right here, and you can't stop us.*

While I'm standing there, Coach Widner walks beside me.

"Watch their quarterback," he says.

I do.

The kid takes the ball from the shotgun. Not under center like us. A running back beside him goes to take the handoff, but the quarterback keeps it instead.

"You see that?" Coach Widner says, his voice gruff in my ear. "You see how the QB pulled the ball at the last second?"

I stare straight ahead and don't say nothing.

"That's called an RPO. Run-Pass Option."

I still don't say nothing.

The Little Johns run the play again. When the quarterback holds out the ball to the running back, Coach Widner says, "Right there, the quarterback is making a read. He's deciding if he wants to hand the ball to the running back or if he wants to throw it himself. And do you know who he'll be reading to decide?"

"Who, Coach?"

He thumps a big hand on my shoulder pads. "You."

"Okay," I say, mainly because I want this conversation to be over. All I ever do is crash the line of scrimmage. We don't play anyone but these teams like us. Teams that like to run the ball. Like to cram it down your throat.

"You understand what I'm saying?" he asks before I can leave.

"I got it," I say, walking back toward the sideline. Just point me at who I need to hurt. That's how I feel about it.

On the first series, the Hanover quarterback takes the ball. It's that same play we watched them practice. Coach calls Rodeo, so Sawyer and I crash the "A" gaps, but instead of sandwiching the quarterback, we find him alone in the backfield, no ball in his hand. I spin in time to see a receiver's hands snatch it out of the air. The kid is too fast for our defensive backs. Touchdown.

"What do I do?" I ask Coach Widner, frantic at the sidelines, realizing now I should have listened to him.

He shakes his head. "We went over this all week, Walker. Make the quarterback choose. Don't blitz until he makes a choice."

I trot back to my spot at linebacker. Sawyer throws his hands out. "What do we do?"

"He says wait," I say.

"Wait?"

But I don't have time to explain. The offense lines up, and the quarterback's cadence begins.

I think about you. Think about you playing Hanover. Wonder if they had RPOs back then. Try to keep in my head what Coach said about making the quarterback choose, but when they snap the ball, there's an electric feeling in my spine. Feels like I'm a lion in the grass. On the hunt. Hunger in my belly. There ain't time to watch what the quarterback does. It happens too fast. And feels like if I don't do something, they are going to score on us all night.

So I blitz.

Like always.

And all night, nothing changes. By halftime, I've got only three tackles, and we are trailing 21–0.

Coach Widner yells at us in the locker room.

"Pathetic," he screams. "You are *all* pathetic! You all quit. Only halftime, and you've quit on the team. You've quit on each other." Then he looks straight at me. I swear to God, he looks straight at me. He says, "Being tough doesn't just mean being strong. It means being smart too."

Sawyer's eyes widen a little bit. See, the thing is, this is our first year playing varsity football. And we've been winning all year. Coach Widner's been *happy*. This is our first time seeing him like this. And it's like seeing a whole new person.

He throws his clipboard against the wall. It breaks in half. Then he storms out of the room. Leaves us sitting there in a circle, our heads bowed. I don't want to go back on that football field. Embarrassed to say that. But I don't want to go someplace where every choice I make is a wrong one. I don't want to go get my ass beat in front of everybody. Then show up Monday for school and hear about it.

We look foolish out there.

By the time the final buzzer sounds, Hanover has us whipped 45–0.

Coach Widner's so mad he don't even want to do film study tomorrow. He yells at us in the locker room for thirty minutes. Says we act like we ain't never seen a football game before. Says we don't listen. Says he's gonna take it outta our hides come Monday.

"Enjoy your weekend, boys," he says, hands on his hips, scowl on his face. "Enjoy your time off. Enjoy it 'cause it's over come Monday. Come Monday we'll watch that film. Watch us embarrass ourselves all over again. Then we'll hit the field, run us some gassers until I feel like we learned our lesson. I won't be embarrassed like that again, boys. Believe me, I won't."

24

Get halfway to school on Monday thinking the whole time how nice it would be to ride that bike instead of walking in air so cold it feels like my fingertips might freeze. That's when this beat-up Chevy rolls to a stop beside me, gravel crunching under its tires. The windows are tinted dark, and a sticker on the back glass shows a boy peeing on a Ford logo.

The window starts to roll down, and for just a heartbeat, I think maybe you are inside.

"Get in, Walker," a woman's voice says. "I'll drive you to school."

It's Sherry Whitmire, the woman from Lukas's trailer. She'd said she'd work on figuring out what he knew about you. So, even though Momma would probably have herself a conniption fit, I don't think twice about getting into the truck. I climb into the seat. Don't bother with a seat belt. Sherry starts driving. She motions to a small white paper bag between us on the seat.

"Sausage biscuit in there if you want it," she says.

My stomach rumbles.

Truth is, me and Momma already ate through most of the stuff I took from that house, along with the food we bought using my leftover cash. And she still hasn't told Coach Widner we need more food. And one thing I learned is even if you eat a whole bunch, you still get hungry the next day.

"Thank you," I say, picking up the sack. I take out the biscuit and start eating. Finish the whole thing in three bites, crumbs falling down my face.

Sherry doesn't talk for a long time, except to laugh and say, "Boy, you musta been hungry. I shoulda got you two of them."

I give her an embarrassed look. I don't like to look half-starved in front of other people.

When we get closer to school, she clears her throat three or four times, like she wants to speak but keeps changing her mind.

"What is it?" I ask her.

"I took that money from Lukas," she says.

"What?"

"I was going to give it back to you, but Walker, I think I need to keep it."

She has no meanness in her voice. She has something else in there. Something I remember from Momma's voice when you got out of hand.

Fear.

"You can have it," I say.

She pulls the truck into the parking lot of a farmer's co-op. "I took his truck. I took his money. And I'm leaving the state. I need this money to get myself situated."

"I said you can have it."

She smiles softly. "You really are a good kid. Don't listen to anyone who says you ain't."

I don't know what to say to that. Feels weird just staring at her. So I look out the window instead.

"Lukas will look for me," she says. "But I can't stay with him after what I learned."

"What did you learn?"

"About your daddy."

I sit up straight then. My heart thuds against my ribs. I swallow hard. "Where is he?"

She takes a napkin from the bag, an ink pen from her pocket. She starts drawing lines. Labeling things. A map. "Go north on Highway 7. There's a turnoff, a county road, about a mile past Booger Holler. The street ain't labeled, but it's County Road 1817. Go down that road for a long time. You'll come to a little stone bridge there. Follow the creek north into the woods."

"What's there?"

"Answers."

She puts the truck in gear and drives the rest of the way to school. My whole body feels numb. When she gets to the parking lot, she reaches across and squeezes my hand. "You won't see me again after this."

"Is my daddy out where you said?" I ask her. Feel fire in the corners of my eyes. I scowl hard so she won't see.

She squeezes my hand again. "Take an adult with you."

"Is my daddy out there?" I ask again.

She hands me the napkin she drew on. "Walker, you got to promise me two things."

"What?"

"You'll take an adult with you when you go out there." She pauses. "And don't tell even one person you saw me today."

I Google it up in the school library. Booger Holler is a little farther up the road than Lukas Fisher's place. The internet says it's a *tourist destination*. We used to stop there on our way to Missouri. Isn't much to it. Don't know if I'd call it a *tourist destination*, but I guess if you're really into hillbilly nonsense, you'd want to go there to buy some apple butter and a corncob pipe. I remember sometimes I could convince you and Momma to buy me a candy bar or a soda when we passed through. I even talked you into buying me a cork gun one time.

I spend all day thinking about what Sherry said to me.

I don't even look at Chloe Ennis through my half-closed eyes during English class.

Sherry said I'd find answers. Said I should take a grown-up with me. I knew right when she said it, I wasn't gonna do that. Who would I get? Momma would tell me to stay away. Mr. Raines would call the police. You would be angry with me if the first time I saw you in weeks I brought the police. Who knows what you've been up to since you left us.

There is one person I can tell.

And one person only.

We watch film from our game against Hanover. Coach Widner just rails everybody. He slows down the footage. Backs it up. Watches us over and over, missing tackles, making the wrong reads.

"What were you thinking?" he asks, as if any one of us has any clue.

I'm on the floor next to Sawyer, just under the screen. "I found out something about our daddies," I whisper.

He looks at me in the dark. His eyes reflect football. He don't say a word. So I go on.

"Wake up early tomorrow. Five in the morning. We're going someplace."

Coach Widner stops the footage one frame before Hanover hikes the ball. "What's going on here?" he says.

I think he is talking about me and Sawyer whispering during film study. "Nothing, Coach," I say.

"Nothing is right," he says, starting the footage. "Nothing going on in your skull."

On the projection, I rush the line of scrimmage, and I realize he was talking about the film. A wideout on a slant route cuts across the field where I would have been if I'd stayed put, if I'd waited on the quarterback to make a choice instead of blitzing him as soon as they snapped the ball. The quarterback pulls the football and tosses it to the wideout for an easy seven yards.

"Do you see it?" Coach Widner says.

And for the first time, I do. "Yes, sir."

"We have to be smarter than that, Walker."

25

Roll up to Sawyer's trailer at 5 a.m. Half expect he'll be asleep, and I'll have to knock on his window. But he's sitting on the front porch, wrapped in an old, dirty Kansas City Chiefs starter jacket.

"Hop on the handlebars," I say.

"Where we going?"

So I tell him. I tell him everything that has happened with Lukas. With Sherry. Tell him how she said we'll find our answers out past Booger Holler.

"What's she mean, 'find our answers'?" Sawyer asks.

"I don't know. But we're going to find out."

I still have a little leftover money. So I stop at the gas station in Dover and buy us drinks. Black coffee for both of us. Sawyer gags when he chokes it down. But I don't. I think about you and how something even as simple as coffee could tell you who's tough and who ain't.

Sawyer's tough.

I know he's tough.

But he gagged. So what does that mean?

I drive for an hour with Sawyer on the front of the bike. Drive until the hills and curves are too much, and I have to stop.

"Can I ride for a while?" I say.

Sawyer nods. We change places, and I hold on tight while my legs complain worse than in the fourth quarter of a football game. I watch the Ozarks roll by. The tall trees. A little house with American and Confederate flags right beside each other. We ride for another hour before Sawyer wears out and stops the bike.

"How far is left?"

"I don't know. We ain't even to Booger Holler yet."

"Good Lord. What time is it?"

I look at the sun as if I can somehow guess the time. But you never taught me that.

"No idea," I say.

"Let's walk the bike for a while."

We walk for what feels like ages. Until we come to an old billboard with a peeling advertisement across the front.

Booger Hollow Arkansas

Population 7

Countin' one hound dog

But there's nothing here but a few abandoned buildings. Grass growing through the planks of wooden decks. Sagging roofs. Doors off their hinges. Broken windows. The website I found said it was a tourist destination, but the only tourists looking for this place these days are crows. Looking at it, I feel sad. Just one more part of my childhood gone. Seems like everything goes rotten over time. Everything.

I start feeling sick in my stomach.

Why would you come anywhere near a place like this?

There ain't anything else to do. I get on the bike.

"Hop on the front," I tell Sawyer. He does. And we press on.

Sherry told me we'd come to County Road 1817 about a mile past Booger Holler. When we come to a dirt road, I stop the bike, wondering if we've come to the right place. There ain't a sign or nothing. Not even a little marker with a name on it. I wish I had a cell phone. All the other kids have them. But you and Momma said you can't afford one.

That's okay.

I get it.

But it would be nice right now to have one.

"Are you sure this is right?" Sawyer asks.

"I think so, maybe."

I pedal down the road some ways, thinking the whole time I ought to turn around. These county roads can disappear into the thicket for miles and miles. Can lead you places take you all day to get back from. I worry if I go too deep, I will run out of time to look for you after.

Sherry told me we'd come to a stone bridge. The path bends around the landscape, and I can't see far down the road for the trees.

We press on. Sawyer hops off the handlebars, and we walk the bike for a while.

Ahead, the road changes.

The stone bridge.

The creek.

My heart hammers hard. I let out a breath. It floats around my head like smoke. I glance at Sawyer, expecting him to feel the way I feel. But he wasn't there yesterday with Sherry. He doesn't know what I know.

Follow the creek north into the woods, Sherry said.

We are close.

We stop on the bridge. Listen to the water gurgle underneath us. Watch little silver fish sparkle down deep. I hide the bike under the bridge. Walk north, following the water's edge. Walk for a long time.

Then . . . there you are.

I saw you
boots toward the sky
your face turned away

I saw you
a fly on your cheek
you didn't move when
it touched your eye

I saw you
blood in the grass
one hand touching cold water

I saw Him
face down in the water
arms and legs in wild angles

I saw you
I saw Him
And I saw the gun between you.

26

They call me out of English for my regular meeting with Mr. Raines. My brain is in such a fog, I completely forgot I had to see him. I take my time down the hallway, knowing he will ask about you. But I can't avoid him forever.

I step into Mr. Raines's office. He is standing with his back to the door, looking at photographs on his bookshelf. He turns when I walk in and gives me a weak smile.

"How are you doing?" he asks, his voice soft.

What kind of question is that? How does he think I am doing?

"Do you want to talk? It's okay if you don't, but I'm here for you, Walker. Okay?"

I don't want to talk. I am done with his stupid talks. I am done with his stupid journal.

His stupid poems.

Mr. Raines said poems can help you feel better. So I filled my notebook with them. Don't feel even one bit better. Don't feel better writing my feelings, whatever those are. Not a sentence matters or does any kind of good.

Hurts so bad I want to pull my skin off.

Want to take my heart out of my chest so I don't feel this.

I open my mouth to tell him *no*. But then everything comes rushing out of me instead.

"He was . . . he was *shot*. I saw his blood. Saw him lying there. His skin . . . his skin white. The gun . . . I . . . I . . ."

Feel stupid, but I can't stop.

Mr. Raines pushes a box of tissues toward me with one trembling hand.

"We hurried out to the road . . . flagged down this woman driving by. Called the police. They . . . they . . . roped off everything. Pushed us out. Coach showed up. Momma with him. We stood in the woods. Everything felt stupid. I hated it. Nobody would answer any of my questions. Just told us they was dead. Gunshot wounds. Both of them. Nothing else."

I hide my face in my hands. Suck in air like a dying animal. Snot running from my nose.

Mr. Raines probably thinks I am a baby right now.

I know you would. You would say, *Suck it up, buttercup*. Or you would call me *Nancy* or some other girl's name. Half joking. Half not. It takes every bit of my strength to pull these tears back inside me. To suck in normal air. To look Mr. Raines in the eyes. Sit there for a long time not saying anything.

"I'm sorry, Walker," he says. "I'm so, so sorry this happened to you."

27

Sheriff Roper comes and talks to Momma at night. I think about Paton's bike right away. Then I feel guilty because I didn't think of you first.

Sheriff knocks on our front door. Says, "Ma'am, the preliminary investigation concerning your husband's death is done."

There's a little bit of tenderness in his eyes, I think.

"Maybe ask the boy to go inside."

Momma touches my shoulder. "Go on, Walker. Go inside."

I try to listen through the door, but I can't hear nothing. Then Momma screams. I hurry outside and see her fall down on her knees, crying into her hands.

"Momma, what happened?" I say. "Momma, what happened?"

Sheriff Roper excuses himself. Says he is sorry. Says he is going to Momma's sister's house to talk with her next. I wonder what Aunt Maybelle will do when she hears. Will she be so far out of her mind she can't hardly react?

I put my hand on Momma's shoulder, feel her shake beneath my touch. I watch Sheriff Roper get in his cruiser and back down our driveway. I watch him through the trees until I can't see him no more.

The team travels to Wooster on Friday. Only time my brain don't feel like molten glass inside my skull is when I'm playing football.

I ask Sawyer, "What did the sheriff tell your momma?"

He says, "She won't say."

"Mine either."

We don't talk about it anymore after that.

We win 33–12.

Eleven tackles.

Four for loss.

I recover a fumble in the end zone for a touchdown.

It don't matter.

None of it matters.

But if you had been there, you'd have talked about it for weeks.

The more I sit with it, the more I start wondering . . . what's the point? What's the point of playing football if you're not here to talk about it, to be proud of me, to puff out your chest at the diner when we eat breakfast and someone asks you about the game.

we're stuck in silence
you and me
stuck close together
but stuck far apart

28

I listen to Sawyer chew at lunch on Monday. I skipped Saturday film study, and I got no clue if he went or not. Either way, this is the first time we've seen each other since the game, but we ain't talking. Not like usual. Just him eating. Me listening. *Smack. Smack. Smack.* He's always been such a loud eater. Grunting and carrying on. Some kids won't sit beside him because of it, but it never bothered me much.

I watch him eat, and he looks just like he did before we found out about you and Rufus. I wonder what's happening inside his head. Is it raging like a hurricane like mine? Is he keeping it together because he knows he ought to? I can't say for sure. But I know Sawyer. My guess is he's angry. Underneath it all, he's angry. He's just looking for the right place to point that anger.

Paton walks in the room, laughing loud with his friends. Chloe Ennis walks beside him. He has one hand draped over her shoulder. And I can't help but notice how happy she looks.

He walks to the center of the cafeteria. Then he stops, scans the room like he is on a mission. His eyes land on us, and he walks straight to our table and sits down.

"Hey, Walker, my pa was out at your place the other day, wasn't he?" Paton says.

"Yep."

"You know what he said when he got back?"

"What?"

"Said he saw my bike leaning against your shed. Told me not to make a big deal about it. Said you were going through a lot. Said he'd get it back later on. Said I'd be driving soon, so I don't really need a bike that much anyway."

I feel the heat in my cheeks. Especially hearing this right in front of Chloe, who I hoped still thought I was a good person. But I remember what you always said. If someone accuses you of something—*deny, deny, deny.*

That's good legal advice, you said.

"Well, that's funny, because I don't have a bike."

Paton rolls his eyes. "Alright, Walker. Fine."

I figure he's done. But he don't leave.

He leans forward on the table. This look on his face like he is just being friendly, even though everyone knows he is not. "Y'all see the front page?" he says.

Sawyer and I look at each other, not sure why Paton is talking to us.

Some of the other football players gather around. His buddies. Wearing their nice Nike sweaters and sweatpants. Chloe stands nearby, watching.

"Why?" I say, hoping he'll say whatever he came to say and leave us alone.

He pulls something from his back pocket and thumps it on the table. A folded-up newspaper. The *Samson Spectator.* He opens it and pushes it across the table toward us.

"Thought you might want to read the news."

Sawyer starts reading, slowly mouthing the words. I read the headline. Read it again. Look at Sawyer, my mouth hanging open. His eyes slowly crawl to mine.

DEATHS RULED MURDER-SUICIDE
By Sean Ingram

We read the article, hunched together. I struggle to keep the words straight in my head. Have to read the same sentences over and over. Because those words don't make sense no matter how many times I read them.

An investigation by the Ike County sheriff's department concluded the shooting deaths of Hank Lauderdale, 41, and Rufus Metcalf, 39, to be an apparent murder-suicide, according to a press release on Monday. Authorities believe Lauderdale shot Metcalf at approximately 11 p.m. on Aug. 5, then turned the gun on himself. At this time, the motive is unclear, the department said.

I don't know what to say to Sawyer. I can't get my head around what I just read. Was that what Sheriff Roper told my momma on the front porch the other day? That you're a *killer*?

Chloe snatches the paper off the table and reads it quickly.

"What the hell, Paton?" she says, lifting a hand to her mouth. "What the actual *hell*?"

Paton laughs like it is no big deal.

"Sawyer," I say. Because I think I should say something.

He stands. Picks up his backpack and walks out of the cafeteria. Leaves his lunch sitting on the table half-eaten. I hurry after him. Catch him by the wrist near the front door. He spins, tears burning at the corners of his eyes, and smacks me right across the face with an open palm. I fall backward to the ground.

"Stay away from me," he says.

I touch my cheek. Taste blood in my mouth. "Sawyer . . ."

He shakes his head. Then he runs straight to the front door of the school, glances one time over his shoulder, and leaves the building.

When I try to follow, Big Belly Principal rounds the corner. Catches me with my hand on the door. He puts his fists on his wide hips. "Don't even think about it."

29

Paper says you shot Uncle Rufus. Then you shot yourself. You took away Sawyer's whole world. Then you took away mine.

But that don't make any sense to me.

I know you're . . .

I know you're . . .

I can't even think the word.

I know you're *dead*, but I can't stop thinking about what that officer said when they pulled your truck out Lake Nimrod.

A problem taking care of itself.

I wonder if they even did an investigation. Did a detective come out like they do in the movies? Did they do an autopsy? Did they chop you up and do math and figure out what happened like I seen on TV one time? Or did they just say *a problem taking care of itself*, call you *murderer*, then go home to their families and never even one time think about how that statement rips down through the news, through the school, through my family, and right between Sawyer and me.

How could two people who run together almost their whole lives turn on each other? And who put your truck in Lake Nimrod a hundred miles away? How did Sherry know how to find your body? Why did Lukas Fisher know enough to tell her? I'm not a detective, but looking at it, nothing makes sense at all. I want to tell Sawyer about it, but I haven't seen him since Paton threw that newspaper in front of us and a simple black-and-white headline tore us apart.

"Are you still writing poems?" Mr. Raines says in counseling today.

"No, I ain't writing anything."

He points at my notebook. "Then why do you carry that everywhere?"

I shrug.

"Do you know what today is?" he says.

"No."

"It's the last day you have to come to counseling."

I feel mixed up about it. I only had to come because I punched Paton Roper in his stomach on the first day of school. I'd punch him again, I think, if I had the chance, so I ain't so sure it did a lick of good. Either way, I'm glad I don't have to waste time doing this anymore. But at the same time, something underneath feels bad. Like sour milk in my stomach. Like, how am I going to keep going if I don't have Mr. Raines's calm voice saying nice things to me every week?

Mr. Raines opens his desk. He slides an envelope to me. "I bet that notebook is almost full by now," he says.

I don't take the envelope. "It's close to full," I say.

"You'll need another one."

"I got notebooks."

He smiles broadly. "Yeah, but this is *your* notebook. It's where you put everything. You *bleed* on the page."

When he says it like that—*bleed on the page*—it sounds a lot tougher than the first time he talked to me about poetry.

"I'm just saying. It should be a nice notebook," he says.

I nod slowly. "Is that all?"

He frowns a little. "I guess so."

I stand. Turn to leave.

"Walker," he says.

He's sitting with his hands laced on the desk in front of him. "Just because we aren't being *forced* to meet, doesn't mean you can't come see me. Okay? My door is always open. I know you got a lot going on, bud. I'm not leaving you high and dry. Anytime you want to talk, I mean it."

I smile a little. "Thanks." Then I start to leave again.

"Walker," he calls. He's still sitting that same way, but he leans forward a little. Gives me a serious look. "You know, *hypothetically*, if you were writing poems, you should consider sharing them with somebody. I know I said you never had to, but you should think about it. Maybe they're good."

"Why would I ever want to do that?"

He looks right into my eyes. "It's like I said. Sometimes the best thing about writing is showing it to someone else, even if it seems scary. Sometimes, we think our feelings are so secret and so hidden, but when we show them to someone, they'll tell us they felt that way too . . . it can be nice to know we aren't alone."

"Well, I ain't writing them, so . . ."

He chuckles. "Okay, Walker. Get to class. And don't forget the envelope."

I slide it off the desk. I am about to leave when he says my name again. To tell the truth, I am getting a little annoyed. I turn to face him.

He gives me a small nod. Then he says, "'It matters not how strait the gate, how charged with punishments the scroll, *you* are the master of your fate, *you* are the captain of your soul.'"

For the first time, something about that old poem makes a little sense to me.

"Thanks," I say. Then I walk out of his room and shut the door behind me. When I get a little bit down the hallway, I open the envelope. Inside is the hundred dollars I'd left under his door a while back, plus a small, folded note.

It says, *NOTEBOOK MONEY.*

30

I stop eating in the cafeteria. I used to pick up a free lunch from the line, then eat with Sawyer. But Sawyer hasn't been at school. And I don't want to see anybody in the lunchroom, either. So I don't eat at school anymore.

Instead, I walk down to the football field. I lie down on the orange-and-navy-blue War Eagle on the fifty-yard line, and I look at the sky. Long gray clouds cover everything. The wind rattles the flag on top of the goalpost. I lie there listening to it, something metal hitting something metal. A little *click, click, click*. Close my eyes and focus on it. Because if I can focus on that, then everything else might go away.

"You okay?" someone hollers.

I sit up.

Chloe Ennis stands on the track at the edge of the field, a backpack slung over one shoulder. I am surprised to see her. "How'd you find me?"

"I saw you leave the building during lunch yesterday. I was curious, so I followed you today." She walks toward me. "Can I sit with you?"

"I guess."

"You guess?"

"I mean, yes."

She drops her backpack on the grass and sits beside me. She unzips the pack and pulls out a sack lunch and rustles through it.

"Are you hungry? You didn't bring food."

My stomach growls. "I ate already."

"You sure? I got enough."

"I'm sure."

I can't figure out why she came out here with me. "Aren't you with Paton?"

She shrugs and tugs the ziplock bag off a ham sandwich. "Not officially."

"What's that mean?"

"I went with him to that dance. He was nice to me. But he's not nice to others. What he did the other day to you was unacceptable."

I look down. I don't want her to see the hurt in my eyes.

She bites off the corner of her sandwich and chews thoughtfully. "I'd rather be friends with someone nice. I've got too many cruel people in my life already."

"I'm not nice," I say.

"Yes, you are. I think you are."

That makes me smile. It's stupid. But it makes me smile anyway.

We talk back and forth through lunch. And the longer she talks, the easier it is for me to find words to say.

"What do you like to do?" she asks me.

"Football," I say. "I got a game tonight, if you want to come?"

"I mean besides football. Of course you like football. It seems like everybody here is *obsessed* with it. What do you like to do *besides* football?"

I think for a long time. "Nothing," I say. "I don't like nothing besides football."

She pops the last bite of sandwich in her mouth. "I don't believe you. Not even a little bit."

"Believe it," I laugh.

"I see you writing in that notebook sometimes. Do you like to write? What do you like to write?"

I scratch the back of my head. "That's just notes for school and stuff."

"Is it really?"

"Yeah, like homework notes and stuff. You oughta come to my game tonight."

"Why?"

"Because I want you to."

She smiles when I say that. I love the fact she smiles when I say that. I am just being honest.

"Why do you want me to?"

I have a lot of answers to that one. But I settle on this: "'Cause I'm good at it. And I want you to know about it."

Coach Widner walks into the locker room before our game.

"Where's Sawyer?" he says. He walks up and down between the lockers. "Has anyone seen Sawyer?"

Paton Roper speaks up. "He ain't been at school today."

Coach Widner comes to my locker. "Walker," he says. "You seen him?"

"No."

And it hurts down deep to say that. I can't think of a time I ain't seen Sawyer for so many days in a row. My cheek still hurts from where he smacked me. Still red like I been out in the cold. I touch the inside of my mouth with the tip of my tongue. Feel the ragged flesh where I bit myself when I fell.

"He lives right next to you," Coach Widner says.

"Don't mean I seen him."

Coach Widner's eyes narrow. "We need him tonight."

"What do you want me to do about it?"

"Find him."

How am I supposed to do that? I've knocked on his door every day since he punched me. I even gone inside once, and he wasn't there. Aunt Maybelle was too far gone to tell me anything. She just rolled over on the couch, said something stoned like, "Don't you forget to put out the fire 'fore you go to sleep. And ain't you forget about our money. We paid in all them years, ain't we?"

What fire? What money?

Only she knows.

"Find him? Why don't *you* go find him? You're up at my house every day anyway," I say.

"You know what your problem is, Walker?" Coach Widner says.

His voice goes icy.

I don't say anything. Stand there half-dressed for the game.

"You lack discipline."

I clench my teeth. Feel the muscles in my jaw roll like waves into a shore.

Bellwork
In the space below, write about your weekend.

_____

Farmington beat us 21-18. I invited a friend to watch. ~~But~~ Bragged about how good I am. And ~~then~~ I go and play my worst game all season. We were weak at the linebacker spot, and coach said I got no discipline.

31

Sawyer turns up at school on Monday. But he won't talk to me. I can't find him at lunch, so I walk out to the football field, where Chloe waits for me. She's alone on the fifty, reading a new book. The cover says *Salem's Lot*.

She closes the book when I sit down, puts it on the grass beside her.

I tap the cover. "What's it about?"

"Vampires."

"Scary?"

"Not to me."

Chloe opens her backpack and takes out two sack lunches. She hands one to me.

"I'm not hungry," I say.

"Shut up and eat, Walker."

So I do.

While we sit there chewing, I think about the football game she came to against Farmington. How I played my worst game all year. I start to feel embarrassed. Especially since I'd run my mouth and bragged to her before the game. "Sorry we lost our game."

She looks confused. "Sorry? Why be sorry?"

"Because I played so bad."

Chloe doesn't think for one second. She says right away, "Football is stupid."

"Stupid?"

"And dangerous. I read this article about concussions the other day, and it said boys who play football and other contact sports sometimes get something called CTE, which is a brain disease. They get it because repeated concussions make their brains look like withered apples. It changes their whole personality. It makes them more depressed, makes them angrier and more hot-headed, and it makes them more likely to commit suicide."

I blink at her. I have no clue what she is talking about. But how can someone think football is stupid? Football is the only time I'm allowed to be myself. The only time I don't have ten thousand things running through my skull so fast I can't sort them out.

"Football is all I got," I tell her.

She stands. Checks the time on her phone. Then she offers her hand to help me up. I stand without taking it.

"It really isn't," she says, as we walk back to the school building.

"What?"

"All you got."

I still don't follow. "What?"

"Football is not all you have. There's a lot more to you than football."

When we reach the school, I open the door for her. The lunch bell rings.

"Not really," I say. "Not anymore."

We watch film during football practice. I guess this is Coach Widner's thing. Watch film on Saturday when we win, Monday when we lose. Guess he can't handle watching us get beat on back-to-back nights. Especially after he swore up and down he wouldn't "be embarrassed like that again."

I sit on the floor. Sawyer doesn't sit next to me.

"Could have used you Friday, Sawyer," Coach Widner says in front of everyone.

"Sorry," Sawyer says.

He sits at a desk in the back of the room and puts his head down. When we turn out the lights to watch film, I think he goes to sleep. All day today, Sawyer and I sometimes looked at each other at the same time on accident. We locked eyes, and it's like I could read into him a little bit. There was anger there. Pointed straight at me like a gun. But a little deeper, there was sadness too. And I know even though there is a rift between us, Sawyer feels just like me.

"Just lousy play from our linebacker corps," Coach Widner says. "Men, this is War Eagles football. That should mean something."

Wait for Sawyer after practice. Lean against the wall for a long time. Paton Roper comes out with his buddies.

"Where's my bike, Walker?" he says, as they walk past. I watch all of them climb into a giant white SUV with a momma inside who looks like she's spent the entire day at the salon getting done up.

The sky is dark. Full of bruised-up clouds. Wind comes down from the mountain. Makes my hair go crazy.

After a while, I give up on Sawyer. Figure he must have hitched a ride with Coach Widner like always. But when I pass the faculty parking lot, Coach Widner's truck is parked in the back.

Whatever.

I hitch my backpack up high and start walking. I can smell the rain in the air. Walk down the long, crumbly sidewalk until it becomes grass. Balance on the curb so I won't have to walk in the mud. I ain't paying attention. My mind in a hundred different places. Mostly focusin' on you.

A raindrop hits my cheek. I stop and look at the sky, knowing then I won't make it home before it pours.

I wish I would have taken Sawyer with me to Lukas Fisher's house all those times. Then maybe he'd see things the way I did. I wish he'd sit down with me and let me tell him what I know. You didn't kill his daddy. You didn't kill yourself, either. Someone else done that. And I don't care what the police say about it.

I'm almost to the elementary school where Older Brother, Mandy, and Roo play outside almost every day, even when it's cold, when someone says my name. "Walker."

The rain falls a little harder.

Sawyer steps from behind the bushes. He doesn't look right. His face is dark, his hair pulled back in a ponytail, his hands in fists by his sides. Thunder rolls in the distance.

"Are you okay?" I ask.

"Shut up."

I clench my teeth. A voice in my head—your voice, I think—tells me to get ready. Says in tones right in my ear like you are alive again, *If he wants to fight, show him he picked the wrong fight.*

I ball one fist. Open it. Ball it again.

I get this uneasy feeling in my stomach. Sawyer and I have thrown hands plenty of times. But the look on his face. The rain. You and his daddy dead. What that newspaper said . . .

I know I have to stop it before it starts going. Or there'll be no coming back.

"Sawyer, I know you're hurt," I say, trying to use the same voice Mr. Raines uses when he talks to me.

Sawyer frowns hard. His lip trembles.

"It wasn't my daddy," I say. "Don't make no sense. Our dads were thick as thieves, Sawyer. It don't make no sense for them to turn on each other. And what about Daddy's truck? All the way up in Lake Nimrod? How'd it get there, Sawyer? It don't make sense."

The rain comes hard then. All at once. Like someone tipped over a bucket. I hear Roo and her sister squealing from the schoolyard nearby. Older Brother hollers, "Get inside!"

Sawyer starts shaking his head no.

Over and over like:

No.

No.

No.

"You're a coward," Sawyer says. "Just like your daddy."

I want to remind him about Sherry, remind him of the things she told me, but I can't get the words out in time.

"You're a coward," Sawyer says again, walking toward me. "Just like your daddy."

Cold falls on my heart. And I know there is no stopping him. I hold up my hands like *I'm not doing this.* But it doesn't work. He punches me in the stomach, forcing the wind out of my lungs. I fall to my knees, but he doesn't stop. I lose track of how many times he punches me. Blood mixing with rainwater. When I fall to the ground, he gets right on top, bringing his fists down and down and down. I shield myself as best I can.

I grab the front of his shirt. Work one hand up to his mouth, try to slide a finger between his cheek and his teeth to fishhook him to one side, a move I've done plenty of times when we were fighting for fun. Sawyer sees it coming and turns his head away.

He punches me again. Square in the nose. I gasp and jerk my head to the side.

"You're . . . hurting . . . me," I gurgle through blood and rain.

But he won't stop. Love and hate are on the edge of a knife. And I know right then he has teetered too far to the hate side. Sawyer looks straight into my eyes. And it's like he ain't there. He pulls a fist back, bloody knuckles washed clean by the pouring rain, and brings it down toward me.

Everything moves in slow motion. Like we are stuck in sorghum. I think I might die here. In the water and the mud. Sawyer Metcalf, the person I have loved the most, might beat me to death in the rain.

Something strikes the side of his head and sends him sprawling. I can't see for the rain in my eyes. I try to stand but fall back down. Then I hear Older Brother's voice boom, "Leave him alone."

"Ain't afraid of you!" Sawyer screams, wheeling around to face his attacker.

"That's 'cause you're too stupid to know better."

Older Brother's white shirt clings to him with rain, showing all the hard-line muscles down his chest and stomach. He sets his jaw and his eyes on Sawyer, then takes a step forward.

Sawyer jumps backward. He looks at Older Brother. Then he looks at me.

"I'm going to kill you, Walker," he says, his eyes red with tears but the tears gone in the falling water. "I'm going to kill you like your coward dad killed mine."

He runs.

Older Brother helps me to my feet. We pick up my backpack, which somehow came open during the scuffle. All my books and notebooks in puddles and mud. My journal is fat with rain, the ink running on some pages.

"You alright?" Older Brother asks.

I touch my mouth. Taste blood. "I'll be fine."

"You sure?"

I shrug. Put my wet things back in my backpack and walk home in the rain.

32

Momma and Coach Widner talk and laugh in the living room. I listen to them through my walls. Listen to them in the shower while I wash blood and mud from my body. And it's almost like you're home. That deep voice of his, accent as thick as bent cedar. I can almost pretend it's you she's talking to, only I don't remember you making her laugh so much.

When he and Momma see me, Coach says, "You been scrapping again?"

And it sounds so much like you. I almost cry thinking about how much it sounds like you. I say, "Just fooling around with friends."

"Looks pretty rough for just playing," he says. But he don't say nothing else.

Momma says, "You got to be more careful, Walker."

I look at them. They are dressed. Shoes on. "Where y'all going?" I ask.

"Town," Momma says. "Going to run some errands. I was going to come get you so you can come with."

"I don't want to come with."

"You do this time, I promise." She has a look in her eyes. Mischievous. Like a little squirrel or something. It makes me curious. And I ain't got no other place to be.

"Alright," I say. "I'll come."

On the drive, Coach Widner says, "Did you know Walmart was started right here in Arkansas?"

"Nope," I say.

"Goes to show you an Arkansas boy can do anything he puts his mind to."

Funny thing for him to say since he ain't from here. "I guess," I say.

We drive the long road to the town, rain splattering against the windshield. I watch the cows in the fields along the way. They huddle together against the rain, using their bodies to keep the little ones protected. I read somewhere cows make friends for life. *Friends for life.* Can you believe it? Two dumb-looking cows being best friends? It makes me sad to think about. But I don't know why.

Coach Widner drives to Walmart. We get out and walk inside.

"Come on," he says, leading the way back to the electronics aisle.

We stop in front of a locked case. Coach calls an employee over and has him open the case.

"Pick you out one of these cell phones," he says, tapping the top of the display cabinet. "These ones right here."

I look around. "Who, me?"

"Yes, you. Call it an early Christmas gift."

Momma holds on to his arm. She smiles at me. Says, "Go on, Walker. It's fine."

I pick the cheapest one because I feel embarrassed. I don't like spending other folks' money.

Coach Widner puts it back. "We can do a little better," he says, picking up a phone with a price tag that says three hundred dollars. "You like this one?"

"I like any phone," I say.

He reaches out like he wants to pat me on the head, but he stops himself. "It's yours."

For Momma, he buys the most expensive phone they have. Then he signs us up for a plan and says he'll pay for that too. "You got to have a cell phone these days, Lily," he says.

Momma squeezes on his arm. She turns bright red and smiles.

God, I never seen her smile so much.

After that, we walk over to the grocery section. Coach Widner tells me to fetch a cart, so I do. When I get back, we walk up and down the aisles filling it with food. You know what he does after that? Pays five hundred dollars for food like *who cares?* Then he drives back to our farm, and I help him load it into our cabinets. When I pull out a frozen pizza and ask him where it should go since our refrigerator don't work, he laughs and says, "Stick in the freezer."

And you know what? When I open the freezer, cold air comes out. Comes right out like it's supposed to come out. Can you believe that? He must have fixed it sometime when I wasn't paying attention. Fixed it like you said you were going to fix it but never did.

33

I hear Sawyer shooting that gun before school. The cold crack of it breaks through the morning air. I sit on the front porch listening to it, then listening to it again as it bounces back off the mountain.

Pow.

Echo.

Pow.

Echo.

Like that. On and on for over an hour.

Wonder how many bullets he has. Where did he find them? How does he afford them?

Mom texts: *LOVE YOU BUNCHES.*

My first text message.

Makenzie finds me on social media, sends me a message: *Had fun, Walker. Want to do it again?*

I don't respond. She didn't do anything wrong, but there's some part of her that represents everything I hate about living here. Everything that is poured out on me and on Sawyer and on every other person who happens to be born in these mountains. It's what killed you. And it's what makes Sawyer want to kill me.

I hate it.

But I can't figure out how to get away from it.

I wish Sawyer had a phone. I'd text him, *hello, I love you, cousin.*

I'm sorry and *please listen.*

I don't say *I love you* often. I guess I'm like you in that way. You never said it. But I always knew. Somewhere in that knotted chest of yours, there was love for me and Momma.

I'm starting to think not saying it is part of the problem.

I pick up my phone, text Momma: *Love you too.*

Sawyer ain't at school. At practice, they stick Paton at weakside linebacker. So now he plays quarterback *and* linebacker. He's the only kid who can play it halfway decent.

During First Team Defense, Paton and I gang tackle the scout team running back. Paton jumps up and slaps my hand like we are friends. Who does he think I am?

After practice, I get dressed and walk outside. I lean against the bricks for a while, my whole body hurting from football. My face still hurting from Sawyer's fists. A sheriff's car pulls into the parking lot. My heart drops. Nothing good ever happens to me after I see a sheriff's car.

Then I realize it's Sheriff Roper, here to pick up Paton.

I look this way and that.

Paton is still inside. So I walk up to the car. Sheriff rolls down the window and looks up at me. He has tobacco juice oozing down the corner of his mouth. He spits into a 7UP bottle and says, "Walker?"

"You ain't right about my daddy," I say.

"What?"

"My daddy didn't kill nobody."

He nods like he understands me. But he don't. And I know because the next thing he says is, "I know it's hard to accept, Walker. But that's what happened. The gun had his prints on it. And there's more, but I don't think you ought to know about it."

"What do you mean?"

"Forensic details, son."

I blink at him. I have no idea what those words mean.

I don't know what to say to him. So I cross my arms and try to look strong like you. "I can handle it."

He shakes his head. "I'm sorry."

"Please." I am begging. I hope he don't hear how desperate I am to know. Or maybe I do want him to know. Because then maybe he'll give in and tell me.

He leans close. "Walker," he says, reaching through the window to put a hand on my shoulder. "You're going to have to believe me, alright? I know it's hard. But we did everything we could, and all the evidence points toward the facts. Okay?"

"No," I say. "No."

Because I don't know what else to say.

Paton comes to the car. Climbs in the front seat.

Sheriff Roper tips his cowboy hat toward me. "Be good, Walker."

I watch them drive away. Then I lean against the wall. I take my phone from my pocket, connect to the school Wi-Fi. I type in, *what is forensic details?* It says it's stuff like DNA, chemistry, and trace evidence like hairs, fibers, and blood. It's scientific evidence. I close my eyes. Sheriff Roper was saying they got scientific evidence you killed Rufus. But how can that be? How can there ever be *scientific evidence* for something I know could never have happened?

34

I hear Sawyer shooting again late at night. The sun sinks down around the edges of the mountain. The trees like skeleton hands grabbing up at the sky. Hear that distant *pop, pop, pop* and that far-flung echo come back at me like a little voice whispering.

Looking back, I wish I'd asked Sheriff Roper about Lukas Fisher. Wish I'd asked about Sherry Whitmire. About your truck being found a hundred miles away in Lake Nimrod. But my brain froze up. And all I could do was shake my head and say no.

I know I have to fix this, to make things better. Have this awful feeling in my stomach that if I don't, things will only get worse. But how can I fix things when Sawyer won't even talk to me? When the police don't listen? When don't nobody care whether or not you killed anybody 'cause you're dead, and you being dead is a *problem taking care of itself*?

Go to bed.

Wake up.

Coach Widner outside, warming up the truck. He says, "Hop in."

"I'll walk."

"It's cold."

"Not to me."

Whole time I'm talking to him, I never stop walking. I head down the gravel road until I hit the highway, then I make the long trek to school, listening to country music—the kind you used to like—from my phone through a pair of headphones. Get to school. Stare out the window at the mountains waking up. Walk the halls all day. See Mr. Raines. He smiles and asks if I am okay. I don't know how to answer. I say, "I'm fine," but he looks at me like he don't believe me.

Walk through my day. My head in a fog. Run drills at practice. Tackles. Heads cracking together, leaving ragged scrapes and smears of facemask all over my helmet. Paton Roper lines up weakside linebacker again. Slaps my hand like we're friends. Whole time I wish Sawyer would come back. That he'll just show up and stand on the sideline. He don't even have to say he is sorry to me. All he has to do is say *hello*, and I'll say *hey, cuz. Love you. Let's bust some heads.*

And he'll smile. Kick Paton out of weakside linebacker. Coach will call Rodeo, and we'll blitz right through the "A" gaps like always, and even though you ain't here, things will be normal and good again.

It's funny how mad I was before, when you were gone and I didn't know why. But I'd almost take walking around mad at you over walking around knowing you are dead. I wish you were here. I wish things were different with Sawyer. I can see now that even with all the things you put me through, there were a couple people holding the back of my shirt to keep me from teetering over the brink.

Momma was one.

Of course Momma.

But also Sawyer.

And now he ain't here.

Now he probably hates me.

If Sawyer hates me because you killed his daddy, then I have to show him he's wrong. You ain't killed nobody. You ain't killed Rufus. And you ain't killed yourself. And if Sheriff Roper won't help, I'll find somebody who will. You can bet all your money on that one.

Coach Widner drives past me as I walk home. The brake lights come on, and I see his license plate glowing red in the middle of his bumper.

It says *Arkansas*.

He drives backward until he is next to me and rolls the window down. "You want a ride?"

I think for a minute. It seems like an important decision. As if deciding to ride with him is like admitting he can *replace* you.

It's not like that, I remind myself. *Not like that at all.*

"Alright," I say.

I climb into the truck. After we drive for a little while, I say, "Coach, can you drive me somewhere on the way home?"

"Maybe. Where?"

"The *Samson Spectator*."

"The newspaper?"

"Yes, sir."

I have this idea. I've seen lots of movies where the police can't solve a murder, but a reporter from the newspaper gets on the case and spends all their time looking into it and even almost dies trying to find out, but in the end, they prove everything and the bad guys go to jail and everything is good again. Maybe that happens in real life. Maybe even in small Arkansas towns like Samson.

"What for, Walker?" Coach asks.

I don't know what to say, so I just say, "Please?"

Coach Widner sticks a wad of snuff in his lip, runs his tongue over his mustache, then drives for a long time in silence. I think he's taking me home. But when he should turn right up the highway toward Sawyer's trailer and our farm, he turns left. He drives all the way into Samson, past the only gas station and to a small row of businesses that remind me of the liquor stores in Blackwater. He parks on the curb. "Come on," he says.

I hop out and look at the businesses. A barbershop. Law office. Maybe it is Chloe's momma? But the door don't say her name. Coach Widner leads me to the end of the row, to a small door sandwiched between two businesses. The door says:

The Samson Spectator

Est. 1901

He opens the door to a staircase. I step inside and walk up. Old wood creaks underneath me. When I reach the top, a woman's voice says, "Can I help you?"

Coach Widner says, "My boy asked to come here."

He called me *My Boy*.

The way you might have, if you were here instead of him.

There are old computers. Yellow with age. A couple desks. Only two people working. The woman who asked if she could help us, plus another old man, who hunches over a computer in the back. I watch him type. The screen glows in tiny blue squares in his glasses. His keyboard is loud, like someone shaking dice in a cup.

"Did you have a question? Or maybe a story idea?" the woman says.

The man in the back looks up. He squints. Then he stands from his desk. "Walker Lauderdale," he says.

"How do you know me?"

He raises a palm. "I been covering sports in Samson for two decades. Been at every one of your games. You're a great linebacker, young man. Stick with it, and it might take you places."

I nod slowly, still feeling a little stupid. A little embarrassed.

"Condolences for your father," the man says. "Do you want to sit?"

"What do you know about my daddy?"

Coach Widner's eyes go back and forth between me and the man.

The man sits on the corner of his desk and cups his chin in his palm. "My name is Sean Ingram. I've also been covering crime in Samson for fifteen years."

"My daddy didn't kill nobody," I say.

"Do you want to sit down?" Ingram says.

"Not really."

Coach Widner presses on my back gently. "Why don't we sit down?"

I let him lead me to the desk. Ingram pulls out a chair. I sit down. There are old newspapers everywhere. A white Dallas Cowboys helmet with a blue star. An old box of Wheaties on a shelf with Mark McGwire on the front. Ingram reaches under his desk and opens a small refrigerator. He pulls out a can of Dr Pepper and puts it on the desk in front of me.

"Walker," he says. "You drink that soda and say anything you want to say. I'm just going to listen to you."

I pop the tab but don't pick up the can. Ingram is tall and skinny with eyes the same color as the star on the Cowboys helmet. His eyes crinkle around the edges. There are deep creases on either side of his mouth. His hair is cut short but messy.

"Go on," he says. "It's okay."

Coach Widner gives me a small nod. I take a deep breath.

"I think Lukas Fisher killed my daddy," I say.

It's the first time I've said it out loud. I've thought it plenty. But saying it out loud breaks it free from whatever cage I've built inside my heart. My whole body shakes, and I cry hard in that man's office.

And when I do, I hear your voice in my head. *Dry it up, Nancy.*

But Coach Widner puts his hand on my back. He whispers, "It's alright, Walker."

I swallow.

Wipe my eyes.

When I raise my head, Ingram looks straight at me. His blue eyes look watery. Yellow around the edges. His mouth creases in a frown. "When you're ready, tell me why you think so."

I tell him everything. About Lukas. About your truck in Lake Nimrod and how it don't make sense because they found your body a hundred miles away. I tell him how Lukas's girlfriend, Sherry, told me where to find the body. And how could she know if Lukas didn't kill him? I tell him I don't think the police looked too hard because you dying was a *problem taking care of itself.* I tell him how you and Rufus were best friends and always had been. How you'd never turn on him. How you and Rufus were like me and Sawyer—

Only . . . Sawyer said he'd kill me.

I tell Ingram how you'd never kill your best friend while I'm sitting there knowing my best friend hates my guts. Suddenly, I *can* imagine a world where you and Rufus ain't friends. Just used-to-be friends. Love and hate walk the edge of a knife. Fall too far one way or the other and you get cut.

When I finish, Ingram snaps his notebook closed. "Walker, I can't promise you anything. I can't promise you a story or results or answers. But I can promise you that I will look into it."

I don't know what I expected him to say, but it isn't that. I guess a small part of me hoped he'd say, *Of course Walker. We've been working on this story for weeks. We'll get to the bottom of it.*

Coach Widner rubs my shoulder. Says, "When can we expect to hear from you?"

"We're a small weekly newspaper," Ingram says. "These kinds of stories are tough because the only record we have to go from is the police report. If the police think he"—he lowers his voice—"*killed himself*, then that's what will be in the report."

"But what if that ain't what happened?" I say.

He shrugs. Frowns. "I'll do my best."

"See, Walker?" Coach Widner says. "He'll do his best."

After that, we walk back to the car. Coach Widner drives me home. The whole way he says, "Damn, Walker," and "You been through a lot, bud," and "I wish I knew how to help you."

I'm glad someone cares. But I don't have a good feeling about any of it. Especially Ingram saying he'll do his best. I don't know how to explain it. It's like . . . grown-ups been telling me they'll do their best my whole life. You with the refrigerator. You with Pa's farm. You with your promises not to hurt Momma anymore. I'm plain sick of everybody's best. Sick of everyone saying the right things out in the open but doing the wrong things behind closed doors.

Coach Widner can say he wants to help.

So can Mr. Raines.

Mr. Ingram can tell me he'll *do his best*.

But I can't believe a word of it until I see something different.

35

S it on the front porch. Open my notebook. Soon as I touch my pen to the page, I hear Sawyer shooting that gun somewhere on his property. *Pop, pop, pop, pop.* A whole clip, real fast.

I sit there and think about the last thing he ever said to me.

I'm going to kill you, Walker. I'm going to kill you like your coward dad killed mine.

Who knows if he meant it. Could be he only said it because he was mad. Lord knows you said some things you didn't mean when you were mad. And, thinking about it, so have I.

But what if? What if he *did* mean it?

What is he doing over there with that gun?

That is what I think about, sitting on my porch. Cold air on my cheeks. My breath like cigarette smoke in the air. Does Sawyer *really* want me dead? Can Mr. Ingram help me prove you didn't kill anyone? And if he can, will Sawyer believe me? Will things go back to the way they are supposed to be, even without you here? Somewhere behind all that, distant and barely breaking through, are thoughts of school. Will we win our football game tonight with Paton Roper starting weakside linebacker? Will I do good in all my classes without getting in any kind of trouble?

All this.

And it is only seven in the morning.

The whole day has a dark cloud over it. I get this sense something bad is coming. Like the whole world is a giant spring been pulled tight. Energy waiting. And something, anything really, about to come along and make it break.

Whole school talking about tonight's game.

We're playing the Pine Hill Panthers, and this morning the newspaper, in an article written by Mr. Ingram himself, said they are the No. 1 team in the entire state. I guess Mr. Ingram's got time to find out the best team in the whole state, but he don't got time to figure out about you.

Everybody says we are going to lose. Even our own players. Right now, we are No. 2 in our conference. Right behind Pine Hill. But Pine Hill is No. 1 in the whole state. I don't even think we got a ranking to compare.

"Something on your mind?" Chloe says when we are eating lunch on the fifty.

"Game tonight. Are you coming?"

"I don't know. You want me to?"

"Do you want to?"

She laughs. "Stop doing that, Walker. I'll come, but only if you say you want me to come."

I get this goofy smile on my face. I can't help it. Every time I talk to Chloe I can't believe we've become friends. "Fine," I say. "I want you to come."

Strands of black hair fall in her face. She tucks them behind her ear. "Was that so hard?"

She lies back, looks up at the sky. Then she rolls to one side, rests her head on one hand.

I turn so I am facing her. "I guess not."

There's some magic stirring up between us. I don't even believe in magic. But I can feel it. Like magnets pulling us together.

And let me tell you something . . . I know I always say *football* is the only time I can let go of the things wearing me down, but that ain't true. Football is when I pour out all the anger been poured inside me.

The only time I have ever been in a moment and nowhere else is on that field, the grass poking through my clothes, when Chloe scoots a little closer to me, a little smile on the corner of her mouth, and puts one hand on my bicep.

Nothing here but her.

Nothing here but me.

Chloe leans forward and kisses me on the cheek. Then she laughs. Our noses touch. Her eyelashes tickle the side of my face. She kisses me again, this time a little closer to my lips. Then I lean forward and kiss her on the mouth, our lips pressing together for one heartbeat . . . two . . .

I feel her lips curl beneath mine.

She's smiling.

Then it's over.

I put her number into my phone. Laugh like a wild idiot the entire way to my next class.

I have nothing to do after school. It's too much hassle to walk home and walk back before our game. So I just lie down on one of the benches in the locker room and play around on my phone. I keep hoping the screen will light up. Say *Mr. Ingram* is calling. But it never does.

I text Chloe: *You still gonna come?*

And she texts back: *DO YOU STILL WANT ME TO?* Plus a winky face.

I stand up and walk out of the locker room. I stand in the middle of the gymnasium. Look at the giant War Eagle painted in navy blue and orange in the middle of the floor. Whole gym is quiet. Like there is magic in it. The same way it feels in a graveyard.

Outside, thunder grumbles. I walk to the doors and look out. Long, black clouds rolling overhead. The front of the storm like the hardened edge of a blade pushing through the sky.

There is a flash of lightning.

Thunder like men fighting.

Text Chloe: *It's gonna rain.*

She answers: *Guess I'll get wet.*

Lightning stops around six thirty. But the rain never leaves. Step on the field for warm-ups. Am soaked before we even run the first drill. Water drips down my face. Dangles off the end of my facemask. I wipe and wipe but can't keep it out of my eyes. Coach Widner wears a plastic poncho. He paces up and down the sidelines and hollers at us. Says, "What are we standing around for? Do we *want* to get beat?"

I scan the crowd. Only a few people sitting under popped umbrellas.

No Chloe.

Seven o'clock rolls around. We sit inside the locker room staring at each other, listening to the rain pound the metal roof of the field house. There are no coaches anywhere, and some guys start asking if the game is about to get canceled.

Eventually, Paton Roper stands up and says, "I'm going to find out what's going on."

I start feeling sick. I look at Sawyer's locker, his pads, helmet, everything inside, untouched. Paton walks to the door and leaves the room. Twenty minutes pass, my guts on fire the entire time. Paton doesn't come back. Nobody comes back.

Everyone starts getting rowdy, wondering if we should go on the field or stay put. Without Coach Widner pulling the reins, we are like wild animals. The sick feeling in my stomach gets stronger and stronger.

My brain keeps asking *what now?*

What now?

Because I learned a long time ago that there is always something worse coming. No matter how bad you think it is, there is always something worse coming.

Coach Widner throws open the door. Paton walks right behind him. Coach's eyes rove around the room until they land on me. He runs a hand over his face, smoothing out his mustache, and right then I know the *what now* is coming next.

He blows his whistle to get everyone's attention. We all huddle up around him. Coach Widner's eyes are sad and scared. He says, "I'm not sure the right way to say this, so I'll just come right out.

There's been an accident."

And I know.

I already know he is talking about Sawyer.

"A hunting accident," Coach Widner says.

My brain checks out of my body. Because I know Sawyer ain't a hunter. Sawyer said he wanted me dead, and I heard his gun every morning for the last week. And now . . . this? My mind flashes back to what Chloe said. About football. About CTE. About . . . *suicide*.

"They med-flighted him to Saint Mary's over in the city," Coach Widner says. "He's in emergency surgery right now."

Everybody starts talking over each other. I look down at the dirty concrete. All my life, I've had these kinds of things happen to me. Pour down inside me like molten glass. Down through my mouth and into my heart, where everything turns hard as diamonds. I guess I got good at being numb. At pretending nothing hurts. But there's no more room in my heart. None whatsoever. So when Coach Widner finally says the thing he's been trying to say all along, it's no surprise my chest cracks open and every awful thing I've hidden inside threatens to break out.

"I have to be honest, boys, there's a chance he won't make it."

The whole room goes quiet. Boys look back and forth at each other.

Paton says, "Let's go out and win this one for Sawyer. He would want us to do that."

I glare at him. Knowing on some level he only said what he was *supposed* to say as quarterback of our team. But also knowing on *another* level, Paton doesn't care one way or another what happens to Sawyer Metcalf. He just wants to *sound good*.

The whole team cheers. Sawyer is somewhere else, under a doctor's knife, maybe even dying, and our whole team is here in a concrete bunker, cheering. *Let's win this game.* As if that's all that matters in life.

Winning games.

I can't speak.

We run through the tunnel. My body driving itself. I watch Paton, feeling the rot inside me the whole time. Oozing from my broken heart through my body. Poisoning every inch of me. Paton smiles and jokes with his friends on the sideline. Like it is any other game. Like nothing hangs in the balance. Like I am not over here burning alive beneath my shoulder pads.

Let's go out and win this one for Sawyer.

Don't make me laugh.

First play of the game after kickoff. We are on defense. Paton gets excited. Tries to slap my hand.

"For Sawyer," he says to me. Right to me. Right to my face.

I grab his facemask and wrestle him to the ground. We land in the mud like two fat pigs, and I can't even tell you what I scream into his face. Paton yelps in surprise. He tries to wrestle away from me, but I pin him down. The whistles start. Coach Widner runs onto the field.

I don't remember much. Hands on me, pulling me backward. Yelling. Paton surging to his feet like he wants to fight me. Like he *can* fight me. My brain on fire, barking at him. Screaming.

Blur.

Like drinking shots of whiskey before homecoming dance.

Blur.

Everything spins around me. But one thing turns clear. Same thing as before.

Chloe Ennis.

Coach Widner hauls me off the field by the arm, and as we push through the fence toward the field house, there is Chloe, standing under an awning, rain pouring off the edges of the roof. Our eyes lock. And I see something in her eyes I have seen all my life in Momma's.

Fear.

Coach Widner hauls me into a locker room. He makes me sit in a metal chair. Then he stands there, wiping rain out of his eyes. He presses one hand over his mouth for a long time. I figure he is about to yell at me.

He pulls up a second chair. Sits down across from me.

"Why would you do that, Walker? *Why?*" His voice is soft.

I shake my head like *I don't know*, but I say, "You said a good linebacker *ought* to be mean."

Coach Widner blinks at me. He shakes his head like he can't believe it. "My God, son," he whispers. "I ought to kick you off this team."

I look at him. Stare right at him. "Maybe you ought to."

He raises both eyebrows. "What?"

"Kick me off the team. Maybe you should." I stand up, my fists balled, the rage that was in my stomach back on the football field returning. "Or maybe I just oughta quit. You know what that'd be, Coach? Do you know?"

His eyes are hard. I know the last thing he wants, the *very* last thing he wants for his precious winning season, is to lose both starting linebackers. "What, Walker? What would it be?"

"A problem taking care of itself," I say.

36

"Wake up. We're going to see Sawyer."

That's the first thing Momma says to me today. I open my eyes. Blue light falls in lines across the room through my window shade. My hands hurt. My knuckles broken open. Crusty with blood. I don't remember it, but I must have hit them against Paton's helmet, throwing punches at someone who couldn't even be hurt by them.

Stupid.

Coach Widner appears in the doorway. He leans against my doorframe and crosses his arms. He must have spent the night.

"Hurry up," he says to me, his voice flat. Emotionless. Like a man with zero patience.

"I'm coming," I say.

I get up and wave for them to leave so I can change clothes. I pull on my War Eagles sweats. My War Eagles hoodie. Then I look in the mirror and remember last night.

I ought to kick you off this team, Coach Widner had said.

And I'd said something back.

Hadn't I?

I look into my own brown eyes. My face still swollen and bruised from Sawyer's fists.

All I can remember is the heat in my stomach. The words rushing out of me. I look at my lopsided face. The scabbed wounds on my mouth. Then I remember.

I'd threatened to quit.

I remember it all.

Coach Widner's nostrils had flared. His eyes had widened. Then he'd swallowed and regained control. "Get dressed. Go wait in my truck. I still have to coach this game."

The last thing I want is to quit the football team.

"Give me your phone," Coach Widner says now when I walk into the living room. I fish it out of my pocket and hand it to him, figuring I probably won't see it again. He wakes it up with his thumb, then starts scrolling through it. I can't see what he's doing. After a minute, he tosses the phone back to me. Color me surprised.

"What was that?" I ask.

"Just checking up on you."

"I don't need checking."

"Ha. Get in the truck. Your momma's waiting."

I climb in the back seat. Scroll through my phone while we drive, trying to figure out what he'd been doing. Or what he might have seen. I don't use it for much of anything. But I did Google up some things maybe I ought not have. Things probably every boy with a phone searches up when no one is around.

I wonder if he will say anything to me. I wonder if he will say something to Momma. And if he does, how will she respond? Will she get mad? Or will she just click her tongue and say *boys will be boys*. Neither would surprise me.

We drive in silence for thirty minutes. Finally, Coach Widner clears his throat and says, "Are we going to talk about what happened last night?"

I look at Momma. She looks right back at me.

"What *did* happen last night?" Momma says, her voice tiny as a moth. And I realize right then she is scared of what my answer might be.

"I got angry," I admit. And maybe it is the first time I ever admitted anything true about my feelings to Momma. It feels like aloe vera on a burn to let those words come out of my mouth. She frowns, and I know what she is thinking. *Walker has too much of his daddy in him.* And maybe she's right. Maybe that's the problem. Maybe that's why Chloe's eyes looked scared when she saw me last night, after I pounced on Paton Roper and drove him to the ground.

"You angry because of Sawyer?" Coach Widner says.

"Yes. And because of Daddy and everything else."

There is a long pause. I expect him to yell. Because you would have. You would have said I'd embarrassed you. Then again, you might have said something like *that Roper boy had it coming*.

Who knows how you'd have reacted.

You sure kept us guessing.

Coach Widner says, "I understand how tough this is on you, Walker, but you ain't doing yourself any favors when you act like that."

I look out the window. Trees zip by. The roadside falls away to an open valley. Grass and cows and more grass. "I know," I say.

We don't talk after that. I wonder if I am still on the football team. As we get closer to town, I start thinking about Sawyer. How he's caught up with that same molten-glass heart I was talking about, how he's dealing with the same things I'm dealing with, only we don't ever say anything to each other about it.

And now we might *never* have the chance since he thinks you killed his daddy. And that's assuming Sawyer's alive at all. That's one of those thoughts that hurts to think. Funny how an arrangement of words inside your own brain can hurt you worse than a lead blocker on a buck sweep.

all the things inside me
like little pieces of broken stone
none of it belongs to us

still it comes to this
     for me
     for you
live with the rubble
or build something new

I wrote that on the drive to town. I tear it out of my notebook and tuck it into the pocket of my hoodie. Think I'll give it to Sawyer when I get into his hospital room. I don't know. Maybe not. He might call it stupid, and maybe it *is* stupid. But thinking about him saying that makes me feel like I want to barf. Except maybe Mr. Raines was right. Maybe Sawyer will know *exactly how it feels*. But that could be a problem too, couldn't it?

He might hate knowing *anyone* knows how he feels.

But Sawyer and me gotta stick together. And even if you did kill his daddy, that don't change a thing about me. I'm the same Walker I was when me and Sawyer were still friends.

We walk into the hospital. Ride the elevator in silence up to the fourth floor. I have the poem folded up in my pocket. My hand on top of it. Ready to pull it out and hand it to him. We walk to his room, and I peek inside. He is asleep in the bed, the blankets squashed down around his waist, his bare chest rising and falling. Aunt Maybelle sits cross-legged on the couch, watching a television program about fixing up old houses. She doesn't see us. I am about to walk in when the phone in my pocket starts vibrating.

It is Mr. Ingram.

I answer fast, expecting good news. "Hello."

"Hey, Walker, are you doing okay?"

"I guess. You figure something out about my daddy?"

There's a long pause. The kind of long pause I don't like. Coach Widner looks down at me. Momma goes ahead and walks into Sawyer's room and starts talking to her sister.

"Well, Walker," Mr. Ingram says. "Remember I told you stories like this are tough?"

"I remember."

"The sheriff says it's an apparent murder-suicide. Says the report from the forensic pathologist in Little Rock backs it up."

I don't understand. "So what?"

"So there's no story I can write."

"What do you mean?"

"I'm sorry, Walker."

"No, listen, you're a REPORTER, ain't you? You're supposed to tell the TRUTH, right?"

"Walker . . ."

"So tell it!" My voice echoes down the hallway. A nurse at a nearby station looks up, raises one eyebrow. But I don't stop. "My daddy ain't kill nobody. Put that in the newspaper. Put it on the front page just like you put on the front page that he did."

"I'm sorry, I'd have to be able to back that up."

I start shaking. Try to pace up and down the hall. But Coach Widner catches me by the arm. His eyes are sympathetic, but he shakes his head no.

"What good are you?" I spit into the phone. But Mr. Ingram has already hung up.

Coach Widner puts both hands on his hips and says, "Damn." Then he puts one massive hand on my shoulder, looks me straight in the eyes, the way you said a man always ought to look at another man. "What can I do to help you, Walker?"

I shake my head.

Because I don't know.

Because what I'd been hoping for was an adult to step in and fix things. Because I thought that's what adults do. I thought Mr. Newspaperman Ingram might figure out who really did shoot you and Sawyer's daddy. And he'd have proof. And I could take that proof and show it to Sawyer. And maybe, just maybe, that can fix whatever's gone wrong between us.

But I learn right then I don't need help. Nobody can fix this for me. I need to do it myself.

Momma pops her head out of the door. "Come on, Walker," she says. "Sawyer's waking up."

Sawyer's whole head is wrapped in bandages. Except his mouth and eyes. His eyeballs move under his eyelids. Back and forth. Back and forth. Through an open space in the bandages, I see they shaved his head down to stubble, I guess so they could do the surgery. All these tubes connect to his body. Machines beep. The light overhead makes everything seem fake.

"What happened?" I ask.

Aunt Maybelle waves her hand dismissively. "Oh, he was just

out there fooling with that gun. They said the bullet must have ricocheted off something. Hit him in the head. Doctor said a little lower, he'd have lost an eye. A little higher, it'd have missed. A little harder, and he'd have been dead."

"You let him play with a gun?" Momma says.

"It's just boys being boys, Lily. Don't judge me."

"And what were you doing at the time?"

Aunt Maybelle looks at the ground. And I know that look. I've done that look. That's what I did when I should have been looking in your eyes but couldn't. When I'd done something to make you angry. When your stare was hot on me, and I knew through to my core that I'd done wrong.

I told him to be careful with that gun.

Told him it was dangerous.

But he don't listen.

Still . . . in some small way I am glad this was an accident. Glad he don't want to be dead.

"He's awake," Coach Widner says.

Sawyer's eyes open. He looks down his body, blinking slow, like he don't know where he's at.

"Hey, baby," his momma says, with a kind of tenderness in her voice I never heard from her before. She puts a hand on his shoulder. His eyes drift toward hers, but he does not smile. I wonder how she found him. I try to imagine it. Waking up through her stupor, stumbling outside, finding her baby bleeding on the ground. Did she hesitate to call the police? Did she wait longer than she ought have, because she was high?

Sawyer's eyes cut around the room. First toward Momma. Then toward Coach Widner. Then they land on me. My hand goes into my pocket. I pull out that poem. I don't know what I am thinking. It's stupid. The wrong moment. Sawyer shakes his head no. But not because of the paper in my hands.

It's because I'm in the room.

His mouth opens and closes. Searches for words. His fists wad up sheets as he presses himself against the headboard of his hospital bed. The heart-rate monitor hooked to his chest *beeps*, *beeps*, *beeps* then comes free and makes a tone like he is dead.

"Get him out of here," he rasps.

I put the poem back in my pocket. Feel heat in my cheeks.

"Get him out of here!" he screams.

The sound shocks all of us.

Nurses rush into the room on account of the heart monitor. One of them says, "I think you need to leave."

Coach Widner sighs. "Come on, then." He puts a hand on my shoulder and guides me out of the room. But I keep looking back at Sawyer. Looking back for hope. Some small clue some part of us are still brothers. But there ain't nothing in his eyes but meanness and anger. Before we even get to the elevator, I feel things shake up inside me. My lip trembles. I fight against it. Not here. Not right now.

In the elevator, I look straight down at my sneakers. A teardrop splatters the ground between my feet. Nobody notices. I wipe everything clean with the sleeve of my War Eagles hoodie. But my brain keeps going ten thousand miles per hour.

Why can't even one thing in my life be good?

Why did any of this happen to me?

Why was I born in a place like this, surrounded by these kinds of people?

By the time I get to the truck, the tears are all down my face. There is no hiding it.

Dry it up, Nancy.

Momma touches my cheek, then gets in the car. Coach Widner stares down at me, his hands on his hips.

Dry it up, Nancy.

"You okay?" he says.

I look at him through tears. Shake my head no.

"What was that you wanted to give him? That paper?"

I can't answer. I want so bad to hide in the back of the truck. To yell at him so he'll leave me alone. To make him know that I'm not sad. I'm angry. And when I'm angry, he better cut a wide trail because I'm STRONG. LIKE. YOU.

Coach Widner reaches out, and quicker than I can react, he snatches the loose-leaf paper from the front of my War Eagles hoodie.

"Don't," I say.

But he unfolds the page anyway. And it is too late. I stand there and watch him read the most embarrassing thing about my entire life. That I can't handle it on my own. That I had to write it all down. And even though I'd planned to give the poem to Sawyer, the idea of Coach Widner or anyone else seeing it makes me want to puke.

Coach Widner folds the paper in half and in half again and hands it back to me.

"It's nothing," I say. "Just some lyrics to a song."

"It ain't nothing," he says.

I expect him to make fun of it. Expect him to react like you would have reacted. But he nods, like he understands something about me he'd never understood before.

Later, as we drive back home, he says out loud to everyone in the car, "You know, it takes a strong person to turn something terrible into something beautiful. In fact, I think that's the strongest kind of strength there is."

Momma smiles. And I know she has no idea what he is *really* talking about. But she says, "That's right."

37

They have a small funeral for you down at the church. They cremated you so there ain't a casket. No body to look at. Just a small box of ashes on a table with a photograph of you beside it. Nobody here but me, Momma, Coach Widner, and a few church folks who probably only came because they feel bad for us.

The preacher stands up and talks about how you were a *work in progress*. That you *weren't perfect*. But that the thing about the grace of God is that you don't gotta be perfect. And that he's sure you're up in heaven right now, staring down at me, and you're proud. Then he starts singing.

> *I need Thee every hour,*
> *Most gracious Lord;*
> *No tender voice like Thine*
> *Can peace afford.*

> *I need Thee, oh, I need Thee;*
> *Every hour I need Thee;*
> *Oh, bless me now, my Savior,*
> *I come to Thee.*

Momma cries hard the entire time. But I struggle to believe one single word of anything he is saying. Besides, my mind is somewhere else. You're dead, and there's nothing I can do to bring you back. So

I have to focus on the right here and right now. And that means all I can think about is Sawyer. And how I have to find a way to prove you didn't kill his daddy, because that's the only way he's ever going to get past this thing poisoning his heart.

And if Sheriff Roper won't help?

Fine.

Mr. Newspaperman Ingram can't help?

Also fine.

This preacher up here telling lies about you. But all I can do is sit here and think up ways to tell the truth.

The Plan

1. Sneak out
2. Find Lukas
3. trick him into saying Something
4. record it on my phone
5. Leave before it is dangerous
6. take recording to the police
   and mr. Ingram

38

Wake up early, expecting to ride Paton's bike to Lukas Fisher's house. Sneak out of my room at five in the morning, walk tippy-toe down the hallway. I can hear Momma snoring in her bedroom.

This is step one of my plan. Step one ain't the hard part. I've been sneaking out of the house for years. Used to sneak out to meet Sawyer. We'd walk down to the creek, sit on the bridge, and pass a bottle of beer or a cigarette back and forth and feel cool like you. Then, I used to sneak out for no reason besides wanting to prove I could. It was like I didn't want to be controlled. I wanted you and Momma to know you couldn't keep me hemmed in, no matter how hard you tried. Usually did that on the nights you whooped my ass. I was too small to fight back. Still am, I guess. But sneaking out of the house and hiding in the woods, making Momma find an empty bed in the morning, knowing she would feel scared, was its own kind of revenge.

I stopped doing it after you disappeared. At least until I started going up to see Lukas.

When I get to the end of the hallway, I see Coach Widner sitting in the recliner, right where you used to sit and get drunk. I about fall over.

"What are you doing up?" he says. There's a cup of coffee on the table next to him. He picks it up and takes a long drink.

"I just woke up."

"You're dressed."

I look down at myself. Same War Eagles hoodie and sweatpants. "So what?"

He tips his cup toward me. "And your backpack?"

"Was going to walk to school."

"At five a.m.?"

"Takes a long time."

"Well, it don't take *that* long. Go lie down. I'll drive you today."

"I want to walk."

Coach Widner stands, groaning like an old man. He walks to the window, the one I broke earlier, and pulls open the blinds. Cold moonlight falls across the living room, and I realize it is cleaner in here than I've seen it in years. At some point, someone pulled down all the old, tattered wallpaper. There are paint cans in the corner, plus a roll of Visqueen, which I saw you use to keep paint from getting on the carpet back when you still painted houses for work.

Coach Widner takes a long sip of coffee. "Too cold to walk," he grunts.

"I don't mind."

He doesn't look away from the window. "Too cold. How about you sit down. I'll make you breakfast."

I sit down. What else can I do?

Coach Widner walks to the kitchen, places his mug on the counter, and starts taking eggs, bacon, and cheese out of the refrigerator. I take out my notebook and go over my plan. This is only the first step, and it's already gone wrong. How am I going to make sure the other steps work?

The problem with my plan is it ain't detailed. I left a lot of room for figuring it out as I go. There is no accounting for other people, no knowing Coach Widner'd be in the living room when I tried to sneak out.

The smell of bacon fills the kitchen. Grease hisses and pops. Momma comes out of her bedroom, her robe wrapped tight around her body, her hair flat on one side of her head. She goes to the coffee pot and pours a cup.

"Good morning," Coach Widner says. "You want eggs? Some bacon?"

She smiles, lifting her cup to her lips. "Yes, please."

I sit there and try to remember the last time you cooked for her, the last time you made her smile first thing in the morning, and I can't come up with one single memory. You said being a man is about being in control. And maybe that's true. Coach Widner *is* in control. He's controlling Momma's smile. He's controlling whether my stomach growls at school on a Monday morning. And that's the kind of control I think really matters. That's the kind of control I hope I can have.

I walk down to the football field for lunch, my hands stuffed deep in my War Eagles hoodie. When I get to the fence, I stop and lean against it. Chloe Ennis ain't there. I stand for a moment, watching the spot of grass where she ought to be. Then I open the gate, walk to the center of the field, and sit down. One more thing I gotta fix.

39

Coach Widner is awake, sitting in the recliner with his cup of coffee, on Tuesday morning. On Wednesday, same thing. Start to think he knows what I'm planning, that he's getting up like this just to hold me up. I have to go through a whole day before I get another chance at sneaking up to Lukas's place.

A whole damn day.

Halfway through school, I get called into another meeting with Big Belly Principal. Coach Widner sits in a chair next to him. Paton Roper sits in another chair across the desk, his arms folded across his chest. He don't look up at me. I think, *This is it. I'm off the team.*

Big Belly Principal says, "Have a seat, Walker."

So I do.

"Walker, we had a long talk about the incident at last week's game," Big Belly Principal says.

I look at my shoes.

"Talked with Paton. Talked with his father . . ."

I keep looking at my shoes. Waiting for it.

"Now, if it were up to me, you'd be off the team. You'd be suspended. But . . . Coach Widner here seems to think the football team *needs* you. But more than that, he believes *you* need the football team."

I look up.

Coach Widner gives a small nod. "Paton and his daddy agreed to let it slide, but only if you apologize for what you did. Things happen in football. Tempers flare. And given everything that's happened, it's understandable. But that don't make it okay, so you'll have to apologize. Right here. Right now."

My eyes drift back down to my shoes.

Saying sorry is admitting I done wrong.

And maybe I did do wrong.

But those words are lost inside me somewhere.

"Go on, Walker," Coach Widner says.

Big Belly Principal drums his fat fingers on his desk. Paton shifts beside me. He don't look any happier than I am. And what's weird is, in this moment, I realize we are feeling pretty close to the same thing.

"Paton," I say. "I should not have done that."

His mouth falls open. He glances at Coach. Then at Big Belly Principal.

Some part of me feels like I should stop talking. But I've opened the gates. And it comes rushing out. "I was scared and mad about my cousin. And I don't know why, maybe because you're playing weakside linebacker where he oughta play, but I took it out on you."

"Very good, Walker," Big Belly Principal says.

Mr. Raines would be proud.

And I guess I'm feeling some kind of way about it too. I feel proud of myself for saying something so hard to say, but there is a small part of me that still feels embarrassed too. I close my eyes and wait for this moment to end, so I can go back to being regular Walker, instead of the Walker who says things that are hard to say.

"I'm sorry too, Walker," Paton says. His voice is small. Like he has to force out the words, just like I'd had to force out mine.

I sit up and open my eyes. "You are?" I ask.

"I ain't been nice to you always. And I'm sorry." He glances at Coach Widner, like *is that alright?* Coach Widner gives him a nod. Then they both look at me like I am supposed to forgive everything.

"It's fine," I say. Because I know I am supposed to.

"Well," Big Belly Principal says, dusting off his hands. "I'm satisfied. Are you satisfied, Coach?"

"I'm satisfied."

"Alright, then. You boys get back to class."

Coach Widner ain't in the recliner Friday morning. I went to bed knowing he wouldn't be. He didn't show up Thursday night. Only instead of disappearing without a trace like you did, he called Momma around nine and said he needed to stay late watching film, and if it was all the same, it was closer to drive to his house and sleep there instead of coming up to our farm. Momma said she'd see him at the game. And I knew right then, even though we had a game that night, my plan was happening in the morning.

When I wake up, I slip out the front door without making a sound. I walk around the shed and get Paton's bike. I pedal down our driveway in the dark, listening to the trees groaning under a layer of frost. It's a long ride through the late October dark, so I go over the plan in my mind over and over.

Find Lukas Fisher.

Get him talking about you.

Record it on my phone.

Take it to the sheriff.

Take it to Mr. Ingram.

I ride past the gas station. Them old men outside, laughing and talking already. Steaming cups of coffee in their hands. I pedal faster. You and I both know in a small place like this, you never know who knows you. Or knows somebody who knows you. And the last thing I need is somebody calling Momma, telling her they saw me riding a bike I don't own miles away from the school where I'm supposed to be.

That makes me think about Coach Widner. I hope he don't notice I ain't at school right away. I know there's a good chance he won't. We play the Anderton Dune Lizards tonight. They are always a good football team. And I know Coach Widner is worried about them. Because even though we lost to Farmington and Hanover, there's still a chance we can win the conference runners-up behind Pine Hill, who beat everybody. We can still have the first winning season in ten years and make the playoffs. Anderton beat both Farmington and Hanover, but they lost to Dover and Steelville. Farmington lost to Anderton and Hanover, so that means, if I've kept it straight, there's three teams, including us, with two losses right behind undefeated Pine Hill with not many games left in the season. Hanover lost to everybody except us and Farmington, so they aren't squeaking in no matter what. If we can win out, we can get a share of the conference runners-up. If we get a little help with another Farmington loss, we can win it outright. That's good seeding for the state tournament.

Not that it matters.

Not at a time like this.

But I am hoping Coach Widner is too focused on football to notice I'm not at school.

He'll notice seventh period, long after I've gotten everything I need from Lukas Fisher. He'll notice when the boys meander to the locker room and get their game-day jerseys. He'll notice when he's handed out every jersey except two. Sawyer Metcalf. Walker Lauderdale. I hope he won't come looking for me on account of the game. He'll have a hard time stopping the run without me. He'll have an even harder time without being there himself to call the plays. But I know even if he don't come looking for me, he'll call Momma right away.

That's okay, I reckon.

By then I'll have everything I need.

Make it to Rushing Road. Stop my bike at the corner and sling my backpack to the ground. Inside is my notebook, some pens, a couple granola bars, and my cell phone. Ninety percent battery. I open the recording app. Check it. Make sure I know how it works. *Hello. Hello. Hello.*

I eat both granola bars, put the phone in my pants pocket, zip up the backpack, and get back on the bike. Lukas's trailer is close. Not even half a mile from the turnoff for Rushing Road. When I get to the dirt road toward his place, I peer through the woods. His trailer is barely visible through the trees. That dog snoozes on the front porch, steam around its nose and mouth. I make it halfway up the drive before it starts barking.

Rope. Rope. Rope.

There ain't any coming back from this. There are about a thousand ways it could go wrong. And all of them end bad for me. But the way I see it, I don't have a choice.

As I walk through Lukas's yard, the beast yanks on its chain so hard I think it might break. I reach in my pocket, start the recording app, and wait.

I don't have to wait long.

Something moves in the window. Then, the screen door flies open. Lukas steps outside, bare-chested in the cold, a giant eagle and lightning bolts tattooed across his belly, some design that stretches all the way up his torso and around his neck.

"What are you doing here?" he says, his eyes bloodshot, floating in the shadows of his face. "Didn't I tell you to never come here again?"

"My daddy's dead."

He don't bother to shush the dog. He comes down from the porch, fists balled at his hips, like he might throw one any second. "I heard. You got one chance to tell me why you're here."

"Sherry told me how to find them."

I watch this news land on him. Move all over his face. His eyes harden even more.

"You knew they were dead," I say.

He don't speak.

I need him to speak, so I keep going. "You knew they were dead, and you didn't say nothing."

Still nothing. My heart hammers in my ribs. Dog going ballistic in the background.

"You killed him," I say. "You killed them both. Then you drove his truck into Lake Nimrod. That way even if they found it, it'd be a long, long way away from their bodies."

I beg whatever God may be for him to shake his head and say *yes, that's true. I done it.*

But he don't.

He shakes his head like he is saying no. But he moves toward me, and I realize he don't mean *no, I didn't kill them.* He means *no, you can't be here.* When he gets too close, I try to get back on the bike, but he catches the front handlebars and throws them to the ground. I start to run, but he is faster. He drives me to the ground with a shoulder. More force than any boy I ever tackled. He pins me to the ground with his knee.

"So what, kid? You think if I killed him, I'd tell you about it? Then just *let you leave*?" He hauls me to my feet by the hair of my head. I punch and kick and scream, but it don't do any good. He throws me to the ground and opens the trunk of one of the old, rusty cars in his yard. I scramble to my feet and run toward my bike, but he runs me down, catches me by the back of my hoodie, and drags me back toward the car.

I wrestle out of the hoodie. He lets it fall to the grass. And I realize running isn't an option. I have to fight. I plow into him like he is a running back. He grunts and tumbles backward to the ground, and for a second I think I have him. I am *stronger* than he is. And he don't want none of me. Then he kicks me to one side and finds a brick hidden in the grass. I don't see it until it is too late. Lukas smacks the side of my head with the brick and my vision goes blurry.

He stands and yanks me to my feet by the arm.

Everything feels slow and stupid in my skull.

He slings me into the trunk of the car. I spin and look up at him. In the movies, the bad guy always says something right then, looking down at the good guy, just when you think he's beat. Maybe the bad guy reveals his whole plan. Maybe he cracks a good joke. Lukas Fisher don't do any of that. He don't even look at me as he slams the trunk and leaves me alone in the dark.

You ever been locked in a trunk?

I bet you have. All the cutting up you did.

I been locked in one before too.

One time I got in the back of that old blue Chevy Sawyer's momma used to drive. Sawyer locked me in there. I could hear him laughing so hard outside.

I wasn't scared then.

Not like with Lukas.

The first thing I do is try my cell phone, but there ain't no signal. I keep the recording going, just in case Lukas comes back. But then, because I think nobody might ever see me again, I start talking.

"Lukas Fisher locked me in the trunk of his car after I asked him if he killed my daddy, Hank Lauderdale, and Sawyer's daddy, Rufus

Metcalf. He drug me by the hair of my head, and hit me with a brick, and I don't know where he is right now."

I try to kick the taillights out, but it's hard to kick when you're stuck in a small space. I think maybe I can force the back seat down so I can crawl through the car. Break a window maybe.

Nothing works.

With no hoodie, it gets cold fast.

I start to shiver. Pull my knees up to my chest. I don't know how much time passes. It's funny because I came here hoping Coach Widner wouldn't notice I'd skipped school. But in the trunk of that car, the sour stench of mildew all around me, I hope he notices right away. That he'll pull himself out of his office, away from football, away from maybe the most important game of the year, and walk up and down the halls looking for me. I hope he calls Momma. Or Sheriff Roper. Or both of them. I hope there are people looking for me.

But I know they aren't.

I've missed enough school by now that nobody thinks twice when I am missing.

I hear a sound outside. Somebody shuffling around. Metal on metal. A key into a lock. The whole car shakes. The engine roars to life. I bounce around in the trunk as Lukas drives through his yard. I hear gravel crunching under the tires. Then the soft and steady hiss of the highway.

"He's driving me away," I tell the recorder.

I watch the signal bars on my cell phone.

No signal.

One bar.

No signal.

One bar.

Then, three bars. I try to dial the police. 911. But before it connects, the line goes dead, and the screen says no signal. Stays that way for an hour. I try to memorize which way we drove. Left out of his house. Left on the highway. Straight for a long time. Then right. Then straight for a long time. Then brakes squeak. Then the car dies.

I hide my phone in my pocket.

"He's coming back here," I say for the recording.

Lukas pops the trunk and stares down at me. Wearing a shirt now. "Give me your hands."

"No."

He lifts his shirt. There's a gun tucked in the front of his pants. "Give me your hands."

"You got a gun," I say for the recording.

He don't say anything. What else can I do? I hold out my hands. He slips a zip tie around one wrist. "Roll over."

I do.

He wrenches my arms around my back. Then zip ties both my hands together like a pair of handcuffs.

"Get out," he says.

I climb out of the trunk. We are in a field. Might have been any field in all of the Ozarks. But this one is seared into my brain, like a cattle iron into the backside of a cow. Burned in so deep I can't blink it away. The distant trees. The sloping hills. The small space next to the upturned tree where I found you, one hand in the creek that cut through the valley.

"You brought me where you killed my daddy," I say.

"Don't talk," he says.

He paces back and forth in front of me.

"Why did you kill him?" I ask.

"I said don't talk."

"If I'm going to die, can't I at least know?"

Lukas spins on me. He yanks the gun out of his britches, but he don't point it at me. "I *said* don't talk."

"You going to point that gun at me?"

Lukas's eyes narrow. He puts the gun in his pants again. He takes a step closer. The whole time I am thinking about the phone in my pocket. I think about how stupid I get when I'm mad. How I do things I shouldn't because I can't think straight. And I know Sawyer is the same way. And so were you.

Maybe that's the problem with all Ozark boys.

We all learn how to be Ozark boys from the Ozark boys ahead of us, only somewhere along the line, everything got messed up. We started teaching each other the wrong things. Like feeding anger. Like being strong no matter what. Like showing people who you are. Controlling all outcomes even if it hurts people around you. So if me and Sawyer are like that, and you were too, then it stands to reason Lukas Fisher is too.

Some folk won't know who you are until you tell 'em, you said to me one time.

And right then I know . . . I need to make Lukas tell me who he is.

"You too scared to tell me what you done," I say, putting a mocking tone in my voice.

"What?"

He takes another step closer. I can smell his breath. Rotten like a fish left on the shore.

"Too scared to tell a boy the truth about his daddy."

Lukas jerks a hand out and grabs my ear. He twists hard, but I refuse to cry out or scream.

"You want to know about your daddy?" he hisses. "Your *daddy* thought he owned these mountains. Thought he could say and do whatever he wanted to whoever he wanted. Thought he could spit right into the hand that fed him. Your daddy was wrong." He turns me loose and pushes me backward to the ground. "What goes around, comes around, kid . . . and your daddy learned that the hard way . . . in the end . . ."

"You was friends with him."

"Don't you see what you've done?" Lukas spits the words. And I am surprised to see tears oozing from the corners of his eyes. "Don't you see? This was over, Walker. *It was over.* And you brought it back. And I don't want to *kill you*, Walker. But you made that choice for me."

Hearing him say it makes it real.

He *did* kill you.

And he is going to kill me.

Everything in my body goes electric. I roll to my knees, breathing heavy, on the verge of crying or screaming, I ain't sure which.

That's when I see it. My cell phone.

It's on the ground facing upward, the recording app on the

screen. It must have fallen out of my pocket when he threw me to the ground.

Lukas sees it the same time I do. Before I can do anything, he snatches it out of the dry leaves.

"Are you kidding me? Did you call somebody?" Then he realizes what is on the screen. He starts laughing. Cackling like a crazy person. "You were recording me? You were recording *me*? Nice try, Nancy Drew."

He puts the phone on the ground and levels the pistol at it. He shoots it three times. The first bullet punches a hole straight through the device. The second tears it completely in half. The third sends a plug of dirt skyward.

Then, as if for good measure, he picks up the remains and flings them across the field. They sail high like footballs and land with a thud maybe forty yards away from us. My heart sinks into my stomach watching them fall.

Nobody knows where I am.

Nobody knows where to find me.

And if I die out here, nobody will even find the recording letting the world know who done it. Nobody will ever know to tell Sawyer he has no reason to hate me. Nobody will ever know that even though you were always cutting up, always doing the wrong thing, always hurting people around you—you weren't a murderer. That was the one thing you weren't, despite all else.

Lukas looks at me. Runs his blackened tongue across his nubbin teeth. "You ready, Walker? Let's get this over with."

He paces back and forth, gun down by his hip. It feels like I am watching from far away, removed from danger, like nothing can hurt me. But watching him carrying that gun, breathing heavy, working himself up, I know he means business. He keeps pressing it against my forehead, rising up on his tiptoes like he means to pull the trigger, then pulling it away to pace some more.

I crumple to the grass at his feet. All of me turns liquid. Comes out of my eyes, and I wonder if this happened to you too. Did you know it was coming? Did you watch him the way I am watching him? I cry hard thinking about it. How you died like this. And now, I am going to die like this too.

Lukas presses the gun to my head again, the cold metal biting into my scalp. I can't stop shaking.

And I don't care if it's weak, I'm not ashamed to tell you I beg him to let me live.

"Please . . . please . . ." I mutter. "Please."

I wait. Wonder if I'll hear the shot before I am dead. Or if I'll just be gone in an instant. "Please . . ."

Lukas's hand wavers. He falls to his knees. He puts his face in his hands, the gun pressed against his cheek with the barrel pointing toward the sky.

"I can't," he rasps. And I am surprised to see tears filling the pockmarks and creases covering his face. "I can't. I can't. I can't."

He lowers his hands. The gun in his lap.

We sit there for a long time. I can hear the blood rushing in my head. I dare to hope he will let me go. That he'll look at me and say *never mind*. But it is a stupid hope.

"I done it," he whispers.

I don't say anything.

"I killed 'em both. Put the gun in Hank's hand so it'd have some prints on it, then put it on the ground between them." The memories crawl all over his face, twist his features. He rasps through tears and snot. "I messed up, Walker. I messed up."

I feel nothing. Hollow. Like an old tree that died fifty years ago, its bones the only reminder that it existed at all.

"Why?" I say, voice small.

We can hear the creek running nearby.

The wind in the trees.

A bird singing.

"No good reason, Walker. No good reason at all."

More wind.

Cold air blusters my hair all over the place.

Lukas's eyes rise slowly until he stares right into mine. "It was for money. Someone paid me to do it."

"Who?"

Lukas chews the inside of his lip. His eyes drift back toward the ground. "I was meant to kill Rufus, but he and Hank were joined at the hip. When it came down to it, I had to kill them both. One thing

Rufus had that Hank didn't. A decent job. A life insurance policy. One someone said they would split with me if I made him disappear."

He is trying to tell me without telling me.

But I can't put it together.

"Maybelle Metcalf," he says. "One hundred thousand dollars."

The name hits like a lead blocker. The air leaves my body. Sawyer's momma. Aunt Maybelle.

"Wha . . . what?" I manage.

Lukas shakes his head. He takes a deep breath. Slowly, he pulls himself to his feet. He takes a deep breath. He is still crying. Still blubbering. Like he feels bad for what he is about to do.

"I'm sorry, Walker. I ain't got no choice in this. I ain't a kid killer. This ain't about her no more," he tells me. "Has nothing to do with her. It's about me. About survival. I can't go back to prison. Walker, I'm sorry. I just can't."

Lukas aims the pistol at my forehead. I stare into that black pupil until it touches my skin, until the hard metal feels like it might break through my skull, knowing the whole time my whole life and death hang on a fraction of movement from Lukas's trigger finger.

Then a police siren whoops. Two times.

Lukas nearly jumps out of his skin.

A voice over a loudspeaker says, "Put the gun down, Lukas."

Lukas wears an expression of shock and horror. His eyes carry a question. *How did you—?* But I ain't inclined to answer. I scramble to my feet and run toward the police car. At the same time, Sheriff Roper throws the car into park and gets out. Coach Widner steps out of the passenger side. I run straight into his arms. Two more deputy cars and a state trooper haul ass across the field, throwing up dirt and rocks. When they stop, four deputies pour out, guns drawn, barking commands. Lukas drops the gun and falls onto his belly.

I bury my face in Coach Widner's chest. I can't believe it. How did they find me? How did they know exactly where Lukas took me?

"Are you okay, Walker? Are you hurt?" he asks over and over, pulling my chin up to look in my eyes. He brushes my hair out of my face. "Are you okay? Did he hurt you?"

They lead Lukas to the back of a patrol car in cuffs. Sheriff Roper throws him in the back seat and shuts the door. He takes off his Stetson, holds it in front of his chest. "Walker," he says. "You okay?"

I can't put together what's just happened. Can't come to terms with being in danger one second and being out the next. So much has happened since you disappeared. So much more since I learned you died. Funny how the whole world can change, can hang in the air like a football, whole crowd watching, their heads on a swivel, the drama of everything floating on that moment, no one knowing what will happen next but everything depending on what does. My whole life has been like that football. Only I never was the one throwing it. I never was the quarterback. Not until today.

I look up at Coach Widner. I am okay.

I am.

40

Sleep through most of the weekend. A few people stop in to check on me. But don't many folks bother. Every time I open my eyes, there's Momma, sitting in a rocking chair she pulled into the corner of my room.

"You hungry, baby?" she says to me.

I tell her I am, but fall asleep again before she returns with food.

When I wake up again, it's Monday morning. Early. Like Coach Widner early.

And sure enough, when I walk to the kitchen, there he is making breakfast. I sit down at the kitchen table, and before I can even say a word, he has a plate of biscuits and chocolate gravy in front of me.

"You walking to school today?" he asks.

"Nah," I say. "Figured I'd hitch a ride with you."

Coach Widner nods, puts three spoonfuls of coffee grounds in a papery filter. He takes the pot to the sink and fills it up. I take a bite of biscuits with chocolate gravy. It is warm. Savory. Sweet. Like something Memaw mighta made when she was alive.

"Coach," I say. "How did you find me the other day?"

That's been bothering me ever since, but in the hubbub of police interviews and all else, I haven't had a chance to ask him. And when they dropped me off at the farm, Coach Widner wasn't there. I found out he'd had them take him back to the school, where he left his truck. Besides, the game was still going on. I found out he'd left right before the game started. Left the whole team to come find me. An assistant coach called the offense while he was gone.

But Coach Widner still had a job to do. Even after saving my life, he had a job to do. I realized that night that Coach Widner isn't in the business of saving me. He is in the business of saving all of us. Every boy who put on a War Eagles jersey while he is head coach.

Coach Widner sits down across from me with his own plate of eggs. "You remember I took your phone after you whooped on Paton?"

"Yes."

"Look, you may not like this, but it's your momma's job to know where you're at, to know you're safe. And it was really stupid what you did. Alright? Really, really stupid. So with you skipping so much school, just disappearing to God knows where so often, and then getting into a fight in the middle of a football game, I decided I'd had enough. I installed an app that tells her exactly where you are at all times. As soon as we realized you weren't at school, we looked and saw you were moving down the highway too fast to be on foot or on a bike."

I eat some biscuits and gravy. Maybe the version of me before almost getting killed by Lukas Fisher would have seen that as an invasion of privacy. Maybe I'd have gotten mad. Let that mad rumble around inside me until it attached to ugly words and came flying out of my mouth.

But at this moment, eating breakfast with Coach Widner, all I feel is glad. Glad somebody cares enough about me to keep up with where I am each day.

41

e read the final act of *Romeo and Juliet* out loud in class. Chloe reads the part for Juliet. I listen to her say words so fancy I can hardly follow.

"'I'll be brief,'" she says. "'O happy dagger. There rust, and let me die.'"

I think, *Damn.* Because Juliet stabs her own heart. I looked at death up close. And I can tell you straight up there weren't even one part of my brain as tough as Juliet. *Rust and let me die.*

God damn.

Gives me chill bumps hearing that.

"Class," Mrs. Redman says. "What are we thinking about Romeo and Juliet? Neither had to die, yet both chose death over life without the other."

Chloe speaks up right away. "It's stupid."

Mrs. Redman nods slowly. "Okay, why do you feel that way?"

Chloe sinks lower in her chair. Her voice softens a little. "Nobody's worth dying over."

After class, I follow Chloe down the hallway.

"I like the way you read Juliet," I say.

She makes a face like I've just said the dumbest thing in the world. "Thanks?"

She keeps walking. I hurry to catch up.

"I'm sorry," I say.

She stops walking and turns to face me. Her green eyes fall on me. They are hard as two rocks. "Don't be. But Walker, you need to forget about what happened."

"We kissed."

"Forget about it."

"I can't."

"You have to."

She leaves me standing in the middle of the hall. Without thinking about it, I put my hand over my chest, over my heart, as if her words have pierced me like Juliet's dagger.

Damn near filled up every page of Mr. Raines's old notebook. Coach Widner drives me to the city after practice. He takes me to a store that sells model cars and boats, paint and hobby things. I take the hundred dollars Mr. Raines returned to me and buy every notebook they have. I have ten dollars left over, so I buy Coach Widner and myself cheeseburgers at McDonald's.

We eat in his truck, parked in the Walmart parking lot.

"Hey," he says. "You want to go see Sawyer?"

I ain't sure. But then again, what was the point of all this if I don't go see Sawyer?

I'm uneasy in my stomach. So I tell him, "Not today."

When we get home, Wyatt's truck is in the driveway. He has a man in a suit with him. Hair slicked back, expensive shiny shoes anybody else would have thought twice about wearing out in the Ozarks. Momma's on the porch with her arms crossed.

Coach Widner glances at me and throws his truck into park. We get out at the same time, and he says, "What's going on here?"

And let me tell you something. I get excited. I don't know why. I think Coach Widner is about to lay down the law the way you might have. I think he is about to put fear into Wyatt and his fancy friend. Make sure they don't come around here no more.

I think he is about to save us.

"He's got the paperwork drawn up legal," Momma says from the porch.

Coach Widner scowls. He opens his mouth to speak, but Momma raises her hand to shush him.

"Wyatt," she says. No sound except the wind and bare trees rattling together like old bones. "I am done dealing with you and your whole family. You Lauderdales are worthless."

"What's that make your boy, Lily?" Wyatt says, venom in his voice.

Coach Widner moves beside me. But Momma stops him again with a raised hand.

"You don't control me. Or him. Or nobody. We spent the last several weeks fixing this place up. We done that so you got no reason to come after us once we're gone."

Wyatt blinks. "Gone?"

"When I said I don't want no part of you or your brother, I meant it. I don't want this place. I don't want to see these people. I don't want any reminders I was ever a part of it."

"So you'll move out?" Wyatt says. He is practically drooling.

"Got a job lined up in the city. And I'm going back to school to be a nurse, like I would have if I hadn't met your idiot brother in the first place." She looks at me, an apology on her face. "I was going to tell you soon, Walker. But now is as good a time as any."

My Momma, a nurse.

It puts a smile on my heart to think about. To know she always wanted something and now she can have it. There ain't a soul alive who would ever dream of keeping her from it.

Her eyes harden and move back toward Wyatt. "Just have a few loose ends to take care of before we leave, so for right now, take you and your lawyer friend, get in that truck, and leave this property. We'll be gone soon enough. Then you can come up here and die for all I care."

42

During a water break at football practice, the team gathers around this water hose Coach Widner had attached to a length of PVC pipe with holes drilled in it. We stand shoulder to shoulder drinking from multiple streams of water.

Paton Roper drinks beside me, making slurping noises. When he stands up, he slaps my shoulder pad. He's been playing weakside linebacker for a couple weeks now. Lined up right next to me all practice.

"You alright, Walker?" he says.

"I think so."

We walk back to the practice field, where Coach Widner is waiting to run team defense. Some boys are standing around with their hands on their hips waiting.

"Heard what happened," Paton says.

"Yeah."

"Look," he says. "Coach Widner and my daddy and me had a talk."

I don't say nothing.

"They got my bike back from Lukas," he says. "I rode it in today. It's locked up in front of the school. The passcode is 4322. I want you to have it."

I wrinkle my brow at him. "Why?"

He shrugs. "I don't know. It seems like you oughta."

Coach blows his whistle to end the water break. We rush toward the center of the practice field.

We have one more game left this season.

One more win, and it's on to the playoffs. If we can pull it off, it'll be the first for the War Eagles since you took them to the state semifinals when you were in school.

So much happens during a football season. So much changes. I wonder sometimes how you made it through and still ended up the way you ended up. All I can think is maybe it's because you never had a Coach Widner. And that makes me feel sorry. Makes me wonder who you might have been if even one person had stood up to you. If even one person had stood up *for* you.

You used to say *it is what it is.*

And I used to believe that.

But I think something else now.

It is what you make it. You learn better than you were taught. Or you don't. There is nothing else.

Coach Widner drives with the radio off. Momma sits beside him, and they hold hands. Their fingers laced together like the stitching on one of Memaw's old quilts. Makes me think about how she made those old raggedy blankets from pieces of scrap fabric. Worn-out flannel shirts. Makes me think about how sometimes things get torn up. But sometimes you can make them into something new.

We drive until we get to the city. Head to Saint Mary's. They moved Sawyer from ICU into a regular hospital room. Momma says he is going to be just fine, besides a scar right above his eye.

"Girls love scars," she tells me. "But don't go looking for one, Walker."

I think she is joking.

When we stop in the parking lot, Momma turns to face me. "There's something you should know about," she says.

"What?"

"They arrested Sawyer's momma yesterday."

I take a deep breath. Justice don't bring you back. And it don't make it hurt less. But it helps. Somehow, it helps.

"Good," I say.

"Well, there's more," she says. "With his daddy dead and his momma probably going to prison, Sawyer's basically an orphan. When he gets out of the hospital, the state will take him into their custody."

"What's that mean?"

There are tears in her eyes. "It means he's going into foster care. Probably in another city. I don't know how much we'll get to see him after tonight."

I can't believe it.

Tears burn the corners of my eyes. And this time I let them fall without shame. I don't feel embarrassed. I don't even hear your voice in my head calling me *Nancy*. "Isn't there something we can do?"

Momma shakes her head. "I don't know. But I thought you ought to know."

I can't stop crying the whole time we walk across the parking lot. I dry it up a little when we pass the junior volunteer inside, a girl I recognize as once of our cheerleaders but don't know her name. She asks us who we are there to see, and she gives me a sympathetic look when I walk past.

At the top of the elevator, I can't help it. I cry again. I don't want Sawyer to go away. I didn't want any of this to happen. But I feel helpless to stop it.

When we get to his door, Momma hugs me tight. "Are you okay?" she whispers in my ear.

"What if he still hates me?"

"He won't."

"He might. You can't know."

She thinks for a minute. "You're right. But you have to try, right?"

I nod. I slip my hand into my pocket. Feel the rough leather cover of one of my new notebooks. The inside is completely blank. Except for one entry. "Can I go in by myself for a minute?"

Momma says, "Yes."

I take a deep breath. Then I turn the doorknob and push open the door. A square of yellow hallway light spills across the room. I can see Sawyer's feet poking up from under the blankets, his toes exposed to the air. I take another breath and walk into the room.

Sawyer's face is turned away from me. He doesn't notice me until I say his name. His head turns slowly toward mine. I watch his eyes drift up my body until we are looking at each other.

"Can I talk to you?" I ask.

He looks miserable lying there. Bandages still around half his face. He nods slowly.

I know what I want to say, but I can't find the right words. So I stand there for too long, feeling awkward. Finally, I say, "I miss you, Sawyer."

I let the sentence hang there, wait to see how he'll react.

After a minute, he says, "I miss you too, Walker."

My shoulders relax. I had no idea they'd been tight. I sit down in a chair nearby. "I heard about your momma," I say.

He shakes his head. "Guess I was wrong. Guess I should have believed you."

"How could you have known?"

He says, "I shoulda known you was my brother." We sit in silence for a little longer. Then he says, "I'm sorry I said I wanted to kill you. I was just mad. I say stupid stuff when I'm mad."

And I know exactly what he means. I reach into my pocket and pull out the notebook. I hand it to him. "Someone told me writing it down can help."

"And?"

"I did. It helped."

Sawyer turns the notebook in his fingers. He runs a thumb across the leather cover. Then, as if he is opening a gift on Christmas morning, he undoes the elastic strap that keeps the book closed. He leafs through the pages. Then he flips them through his thumb like a deck of cards.

"I wrote something on the first page for you," I say.

He turns back the pages. "What is it?"

"It's a poem. For you."

Outside, two nurses laugh at some unheard joke. A woman walks by holding a bouquet of flowers. Momma pokes her head in the door, then disappears. I watch Sawyer's lips move as he reads the poem to himself. When he finishes, he doesn't look up. Then he reads it again. Right out loud.

I wipe a tear out of my eyes and wonder if this might be our last moment together.

Sawyer closes the book. "You know what, Walker?" he says.

"What?"

"I feel that same way. I didn't even know it until you put words to it, but I've felt like that, just like that, my whole life."

"Well, you can have that notebook."

Sawyer holds the book to his chest. He closes his eyes. And when he opens them again, he smiles his crooked, missing-tooth smile.

"Thanks, Walker," he says. "Thanks."

43

I step into Mr. Raines's office. He looks up from his computer and smiles. "Walker, how have you been?"

Already I can see he is shaking more. There are bottles of medicine on the table next to him, and somewhere deep in his eyes, I can see pain. Like he is being hit blindside by a pulling guard nonstop.

"Good and bad," I say.

"You want to sit?"

I close the door and sit down across from him.

"I heard about everything," he says.

I nod. "It's been tough. Are . . . you okay?"

"Me? Walker, I'm fine. Don't worry about me. I can't imagine what you're going through."

We sit in silence for a minute, the clock ticking. I came in here for a reason, but now it's tough to find the words to explain to him how I'm feeling.

"Do you need help with something . . . or?" he coaxes.

So I tell him everything. I tell him about Sawyer and how we fought. And how I fought to make sure he knew he and I were family, but now it seems like he is going to go into foster care anyway and I might never see him again. I tell him how Lukas Fisher pressed that gun right into my head, and sometimes I wake up in the middle of the night and feel the way it cut into my skin. Sometimes I see his face, think maybe he got out of the county jail and is looking for me.

I tell him about Chloe and how she kissed me but now she won't talk to me at all.

I cry in his office and don't feel ashamed of it.

"This shit is hard," I tell him.

"You got more going on than most people realize," Mr. Raines says.

"I thought maybe Chloe could realize."

"She's got to do what's right for herself."

"What should I do?"

"Tell her how you feel."

"What if she still don't want to be around me?"

Mr. Raines nods slowly. "Then you'll have to accept it, Walker. Accepting things you can't control takes real strength. I know that's hard, but you can't force things. Forcing things only makes it worse."

It's almost time for my next class. I stand up. Say, "Are you sure you're okay?"

"I'm fine, buddy. Thank you for asking."

At lunch, I skip the football field. I keep thinking about the time Chloe said there was a lot more to me than football. At the time, I couldn't see it. But now . . . I know she's right. I like writing in this notebook. I like putting together poems. I think I might even take that creative writing class I saw on Chloe's notebook.

I go to the library.

The librarian, a humpbacked old woman named Mrs. Lunney, looks at me like I am the last person on the planet she expected to see in the library during lunch break.

"Can I help you?" she asks.

"I was wondering if you knew about any good poetry books," I say.

"The Dr. Seuss books are at the elementary school," she says.

Somehow, I let myself forget who these people think I am.

It's like I'm carrying around a secret fire. Sometimes, it's the only thing keeping me warm, but some people want to pour water on it anyway.

I walk around the edge of the library, looking at the titles.

There's a poster between shelves titled *DEWEY DECIMAL SYSTEM* that says poetry books start in the 800s, so I walk around watching the numbers grow on the spines. When I find them, I grab a book of collected poems by Emily Dickinson. Another by someone called e.e. cummings. I have no idea who either is, but I take the books to the front desk and place them on the counter.

Mrs. Lunney looks at the titles. "You like poetry?"

I nod.

"Hold on a second." Mrs. Lunney walks across the room to the poetry section. She grabs a book and carries it to me. She sticks it on top of the stack. The cover says *Selected Poems by Robert Frost*.

"Try this one too," she says. "It's my favorite."

She scans the books into the computer. Says I have to return them in two weeks.

I don't bother stuffing them in my backpack. I don't care who sees them.

Tomorrow we play with a chance to clinch a playoff berth. I try to focus my brain on it all day. Try to go back in my memory and think about all the times Coach Widner told us, *This is goal number one. Qualify for the state tournament. From there . . . who knows?*

But all I can think about is Chloe.

Mrs. Redman steps out of the room during English. The whole room buzzes as students begin talking to one another. Chloe takes out a book and starts reading. This time it ain't *Salem's Lot*. The cover says *The Shining*.

"Is it good?" I ask.

"I just started it."

I lean a little closer. This is the first time she's spoke to me since she told me to *forget it*. As if I ever can forget that tiny sacred moment between us. "Can I talk to you?"

She closes the book. "What do you want to talk about, Walker?"

I think back to what Mr. Raines said earlier. It seems like I have this one chance, like a desperation pass with thirty seconds left in the game. You either catch it and celebrate, or it hits the ground and it's over.

Tell her how you feel . . .

Mr. Raines's voice in my head.

Tell . . . her . . .

"I like you," I say. "I like being around you."

Chloe looks right in my eyes. She don't break away one time. But when she doesn't speak, I look down at my desk. "Anyway."

A long moment passes. My heart lurches in my chest. Mr. Raines told me to tell her how I feel, but he didn't tell me I would feel so raw and exposed. Like she can see straight through me. See my heart vibrating. Like I ain't wearing any skin at all.

"Walker," she says, finally.

My eyes meet hers. I wait.

"I lied," she says.

"About what?"

"Remember I said I moved here because my mom is a lawyer and we came here because she wanted to live where she grew up?"

"Yeah."

"Not true."

"I don't care, Chloe. It's alright you lied. I've lied a lot of times in my life."

"No, Walker, listen . . ."

I shut up and listen.

"We moved from Aurora because my dad beat up my mom two years ago. He got sent to prison, and we thought that was the end of it, but last summer he started sending us letters and calling our phones. He said he was up for parole. He said he thought he'd get out on *good behavior*. He said he was going to come home, but there was this . . . undercurrent to everything, like it was a threat. So Mom threw a dart at a map, and we packed our things. We changed our phone numbers and left the next week. We came here. And after all that . . . I met you."

I frown. I'm not sure where she's going with this, but I reckon I won't like it when she gets there.

"So believe me when I tell you this: I will not spend any time with anybody who is anything like my father. I thought you might have been different. Might have been one of the good ones. And maybe you *will* be one day, but when I saw you jump Paton on the football field, all I saw was my father hitting my mother."

"I'm not like that," I say. My voice cracks right down the middle.

She stares right at me. I swear to God, it's as if she isn't blinking. "No, Walker. I'm sorry. But no."

I don't say anything for the rest of class. I keep thinking there has to be something I can do or say to win her over. In the hallway, I hurry to walk beside her. "Remember you asked me what I like besides football?"

I can tell she is annoyed.

"I like writing poems." I lift my notebook to show her.

Her eyes soften some. I can see tears in them. I have hope. For just a second, I have hope.

"That's great, Walker," she says. "But my answer is still no."

She walks away then. I stand there in the hall. My conversation with Mr. Raines comes back to me.

What if she still don't want to be around me?

Then you'll have to accept it.

That takes strength.

There is one line in this book by e.e. cummings I like. I don't know what it means, but I like it.

In thy beauty is the dilemma of flutes.

I don't know why, but it makes me think of Chloe.

It's nice this afternoon. Still cold, but warmer than it's been in a week or more. The October sun low in a cloudless sky. Coach Widner waits by the truck, but I tell him I want to walk.

"You want to walk?" he says, his hands in his pockets. "You sure?"

"It's nice out. The air feels good in my lungs."

"We can roll the windows down," he says. "Come on."

And I can tell there ain't no stopping him. I don't have a phone again yet, so there ain't no kind of tracking software to keep up with me. Truth is, I don't think Coach Widner or Momma all the way trust me yet. Not that I all the way blame them.

I hop in the truck, and Coach Widner hits the gas. We drive the same way I always walk. There ain't no other way to go. We drive alongside the sidewalk until it crumbles into tall grass. Then we turn next to the elementary school. I look across the playground, where Older Brother stands watch over his sisters. He's wearing his jacket. Roo's got on a puffer coat and a pair of jeans, a pair of rubber rain boots. Mandy's wearing a War Eagles hoodie, several sizes too big, but it seems like that's a fashion statement more than anything else. She got on blue jeans and a pair of real cowboy boots. Roo runs from one end of the playground to the other, screaming and flailing her arms. Mandy doubles over, laughing harder than I've ever seen anyone laugh. On the pavement, its little pinchers waving angrily in the air, a crawdad scoots backward toward the muddy grass. Older Brother glances up at our truck as we drive past. But I don't think he can see me through the tinted windows.

44

Coach Widner drives the long road to the city so we can visit with Sawyer. Momma says since his momma got arrested, he just been sitting up there alone.

"That ain't good for nobody," she says.

And I agree.

I wonder if he's written anything in that notebook I gave him. Lord knows he's got the time these days. Last time I came and saw him, he hadn't written a damn thing. He said, "I look at the page, and it's like my whole brain freezes. Nothing comes out."

Funny talking to him. It's the same old Sawyer as ever. But . . . I don't know how to explain it. The love that's always been between us is right out in the open. When I saw him last, he said, "I love you, cuz." And I said it back. And he said, "I mean it." And I said, "I mean it too."

And that is the first time we ever had a conversation like that.

I'm looking forward to seeing him today.

Coach Widner plays blues music on the stereo as we drive to the city, moving his fingers on the steering wheel like he's playing the electric guitar. He laughs and jokes, and Momma does too. I've never seen him this happy. Like a kid. A silly kid. And Momma is too.

When we get to the hospital, they hold hands walking inside. Like a couple of love birds. Like teenagers. It's funny. Momma reaches down with her other hand and takes mine, and we walk that way in a single line. Some guys don't wanna be seen holding hands with they momma. But I am not one of those people.

We take the stairs because Momma's been on a fitness kick lately. Sawyer's on the third floor, so Momma and Coach are huffing and puffing by the time we get to the waiting room. We walk down the hallway. Coach Widner says, still catching his breath, "Jesus, Lily, you gonna kill me with this fitness crap."

Halfway to Sawyer's room, I start glancing through doors. I know I'm seeing private moments inside these hospital rooms, but I can't help it. Families huddled together. Nurses helping folks. I am in awe of the countless ways folks take care of each other. It ain't all hardness in this world. Not all the time.

In one room, a man is asleep in the center of the room. An older man sits in a chair nearby, one leg hitched over the other, his nose buried in a book. He looks up when I peek in. I don't recognize him.

But the man in the bed—

"Mr. Raines?" I say.

"The elder," the man sitting nearby says. "Are you one of my son's students?"

"What's wrong with him?"

Momma stops walking a few strides ahead of me. She comes back and stands behind me, her hand touching the back of my neck.

"Oh, hey, Walker," Mr. Raines says, his eyes opening. He starts to sit up, but gives up halfway. His father rises to prop a pillow behind his neck. "You don't have to stand in the door. You can come in here."

"Are you okay?" I ask.

"For the moment, I guess."

"You guess?" I take a few steps into the room. He looks thinner than I remember, even though it ain't been that long since I last saw him. Sleepier. Like he's been through the ringer. "What's going on?"

He and his father share a silent conversation. Then Mr. Raines's head swivels back toward me. "I have amyotrophic lateral sclerosis."

"You have what?"

"ALS, you probably heard it called. Or maybe Lou Gehrig's Disease? Remember that ice bucket challenge a few years back?"

I don't have a clue what he's talking about.

"You'll be okay though, right?" The two men look at each other again. "Right?"

"Well . . . it's a disease that impairs how my brain communicates with my body. My muscles will get weak. They'll atrophy. Eventually, I won't be able to walk or stand. I won't be able to eat. It will gradually make me weaker and weaker and weaker." Mr. Raines pauses, collects his thoughts. Then his eyes cut toward mine. "This will kill me, Walker."

He says it so plain. Like he isn't afraid. Like he is Juliet with her dagger. I walk a little closer and stand beside his bed.

He looks up at me and says, "I'm real proud of you, Walker."

"Proud?"

"Some folks go their whole lives and never do battle with themselves. It never occurs to them that their whole worldview is wrong."

"Why are you saying this?" My throat hurts from trying not to cry.

"Because I'm not coming back to school. And I may not get another chance to say it. And you need to hear it. I'm so glad you happened by here today."

I look at his father. The other Mr. Raines. He is crying without shame. And that seems to give me permission. This stupid man I hated so much tricked me into loving him. He ain't even kin, and I love him. One of the few folks in this whole world who saw the good in me. He saw it when I couldn't even see it in myself.

Mr. Raines laughs suddenly.

"Hey," he says. "I'm not going anywhere today. I'm *fine* today. In this moment. Right now. Isn't that all anyone really has? How is your writing going? Did you talk to Chloe? What about you and Sawyer? I heard he was getting better."

And on like that, asking questions and questions.

I sit down at the edge of the bed. His hand is on the outside of the covers, so I hold it.

Momma says, "I'll walk over and see Sawyer. Take your time, Walker."

45

The Haggerton Blue Devils kick us the ball to start the game.

The whole time I watch the ball sail high in the air, I think, *One more win. One more, and then it's playoff season.*

Paton returns the kick to the thirty, then waits for the offense to take the field. I stand beside Coach Widner, in case he needs me to play halfback in our old, hard-nosed Dead-T offense.

Haggerton has only won three games this year. On paper, it's an easy win. But you know and I know *on paper* and *real life* are two different things.

Before the game, Coach Widner tells us, "Don't let their record fool you. This is a good football team, playing in one of the toughest conferences in all of Arkansas. You go out there and handle business, and we get to play more football. You go out there and play like they're soft, and they'll punch you in the mouth, I can promise you that. They'll punch you in the mouth, and your season is over. I don't know about you, but I want to play more football."

From the start of the year, one of our main goals has been to have the first winning season in Samson in ten years. If we can win tonight, we'll accomplish that. But better than that, a win tonight means playoffs. And Coach Widner says playoffs are a whole new season.

"In the playoffs, it don't matter what your record is. One loss, and you are done. It's a whole new season, and everyone is 0–0," he told us during practice this week.

You would have been beside yourself with pride over this whole thing.

I turn and look at the stands. It's full of mommas and daddies screaming. My momma's near the top, her Samson War Eagles sweater on. Used to be, she always sat beside you and Aunt Maybelle.

But not anymore.

And I can't lie, I feel the blank space in the bleachers where you ought to be.

It's still heavy on me.

This morning, Momma woke me up early. "Come on, get breakfast," she said. "I got something to talk to you about."

At the time, I thought she was going to tell me her and Coach Widner were getting married. And if you'd have told me that a few weeks ago, I might have gone through the roof. But thinking about them getting married put a little smile on my heart instead. Momma ought to be happy. And if you ever loved her, you'd agree.

Momma had a plate of eggs and pancakes on the table. "We're moving into a duplex closer to your school," she said.

"Is that the news?"

She laughed. "No."

"Then what is it, Momma? You getting married?"

She laughed even harder. "Walker, please. Me and Andre only been together for a little while."

"Well, what is it?"

"What do you think about sharing your bedroom?"

"I don't think about it. Why would I think about it?"

"Well . . ." She sat down across from me. "The case worker said we're the closest family Sawyer's got. Said we might could adopt him."

My mouth fell open.

"If nothing else, they said he can live with us until things get figured out."

"We'd be like brothers," I said.

"You already are like brothers," she said.

The band plays the fight song, and I snap back into the moment just before the first play of the first quarter. Paton slides his hands under center. He hollers "Hike!" and bodies slam together at the line of scrimmage. Paton runs a quarterback keeper, slips past two defenders, and chugs fifty yards to the end zone. The crowd surges to their feet, clapping and hollering. Coach goes for the two-point conversion and we go up 8–0 in a flash.

After we kick the ball, I walk out on the field.

My turn.

I line up at strongside linebacker, Paton beside me. He reaches out his hand. And I slap it hard.

"Let's get this," I tell him. He nods. Gives me a small grin. Coach dials up Rodeo, and we crash through the "A" gaps, sandwich Haggerton Quarterback between our helmets.

Haggerton runs to the weak side next play. Paton and the corner swallow the running back near the sideline. Third down.

Haggerton Quarterback drops back. A running back slips through the line, dashing straight toward me. He makes a cut, and I follow, just as Haggerton Quarterback flips the ball forward, his fingers curling in the air like he's pointing at something far away.

And in my head, I know, there in the first quarter, this game is over.

The ball sails right into my chest. I don't even have to try and catch it.

And then . . . the field opens before me. Not a person alive can stop me from finding that end zone. When I cross the goal line, I spin toward the crowd. Coach Widner is screaming. Momma is screaming. I hold the ball high. Hold it toward the sky.

I hold it there for you.

READING GUIDE

1. What is the major theme of *Strong Like You*, and how does Walker's journey tie into it?
2. Why does Walker struggle with anger issues?
3. How is strength explored in the secondary characters? How is Mr. Raines strong? How is Coach Widner strong? How is Walker's mother strong? How is Older Brother strong? How is Chloe strong?
4. Which characters are the negative portrayals of strength in this story, and in what ways are their portrayals of strength harmful?
5. How does writing in a journal help Walker?
6. Why do you think Mr. Raines shared "Invictus" with Walker? How does the poem tie into the theme of the book?
7. Why is Walker immediately drawn to Chloe? Why does Walker ultimately reject Makenzie?
8. Why does Chloe decide she cannot be with Walker?
9. Why does Walker ultimately decide to stop pursuing Chloe? Why might this be an important sign of his growth?
10. What do Walker's handwritten bellwork assignments reveal about his character?
11. Why do you think Walker was drawn to football?
12. How does football relate to the theme of the book?
13. Does Walker end the book in a better place than where he started? How so?
14. Was there a moment, passage, or sentence in this book that impacted you? What was it, and why did it stand out to you?
15. If you could ask the author a question, what would you ask him?

ACKNOWLEDGMENTS

When I set out to write *Strong Like You*, I knew I had a lot to say about masculinity—both the regular and toxic variety. I asked myself what I would say to the sensitive young boys of the world, the ones who have been crammed into a "this is what it means to be a man" box that in no way, shape, or form resembles what it actually means to be a man.

In other words, what would I say to boys like me?

Now that the work is complete, I have to acknowledge those who helped me grow into what I grew into. It took a long time. Maybe too long, but I think I finally have my head on straight.

I have to thank my mother and my father. My own parents were nothing like Walker's. My home had traditional ideas, yet I was never prohibited from reading any book I had an interest in. I became a lifelong lover of the written word and of stories. I was allowed and encouraged to explore my creative side from the moment my parents knew I had one. My father made sure I never lacked notebooks or pencils to write in them.

I have to thank my wife, who pushed me over ten years ago to ask for more work at the local paper—a move that led to a gig covering local sports. Thank you to my first editors, Sean Ingram and Mike Roark, who gave me a chance when I wanted more than anything to write words for a living. I covered not only sports, but crime, feature stories, city and state government—you name it—until eventually, I took over as managing editor of the paper. None of that would have happened without my wife, Melissa. I often joke her journalism degree paid for both our educations. It's funny because it's true.

Thank you to the members of ARDWC: Eli Cranor, Joshua Wilson, and John Post. Your encouragement and advice changed everything. To my agent, Shari Maurer—you were the first to believe in my fiction writing, and your guidance and hard work has been second to none. To my editor, Meg Gaertner, and all the others who put in countless hours of hard work at Flux to make this happen. Thank you for seeing Walker exactly as I imagined him, and thank you for seeing how important it was for his voice to be shared with the world.

Thank you to my kids—Greg, Kaylee, Jeffrey, and Henry. You all inspire me daily. Thank you to my old creative writing teacher, Teddie Faye Raines; to Shaun Hamill and any other professional writers who were happy to talk and encouraged me (and inscribed kind things to me in their books). Thank you to Cade Hagen, who read this and other manuscripts of mine . . . You're next!

To my readers, both new and old: Thank you for your kind words over the years, your attention, your feedback, and your support. It means more to me than you can know.

ABOUT THE AUTHOR

T. L. Simpson is an award-winning journalist living in Arkansas. He is currently the editor of his hometown paper. His fiction draws from his experiences growing up in the Ozarks and his years of journalism covering both sports and crime. Simpson lives in the Arkansas River Valley, between the Ozark and Ouachita Mountains, with his wife and four kids.